W9-AAF-499

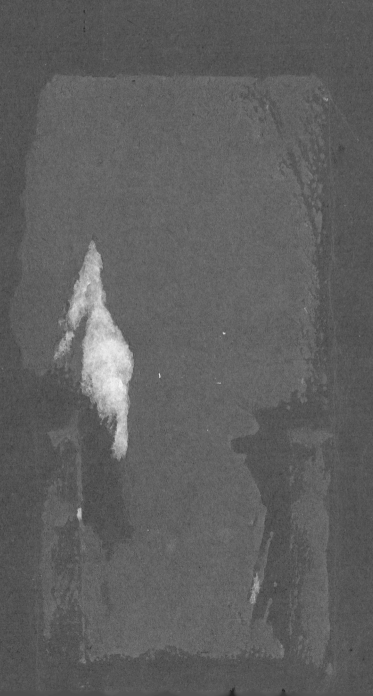

The Liberation of
Clementine Tipton

Books by
JANE FLORY

Clancy's Glorious Fourth
Faraway Dream
Mist on the Mountain
One Hundred and Eight Bells
Peddler's Summer
Ramshackle Roost
A Tune for the Towpath
We'll Have a Friend for Lunch

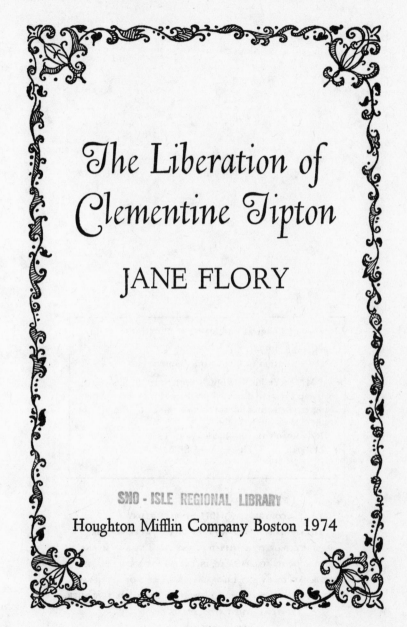

The Liberation of Clementine Tipton

JANE FLORY

Houghton Mifflin Company Boston 1974

Library of Congress Cataloging in Publication Data

Flory, Jane, 1917–
    The liberation of Clementine Tipton.

    SUMMARY: Philadelphia's centennial celebration in
1876 and the activities of a growing women's movement
bring excitement and some new ideas to the life of
young Clementine Tipton.
    [1. Women's rights—Fiction] I. Title.
PZ7.F665Li   [Fic]   74–8180
ISBN 0–395–19493–8

J
FLORY
1974

Dedicated to the peculiar, impossible, aggravating
and somehow lovable institution that has meant
so much to me. Founded as the School of Industrial
Arts in 1876 as a direct outgrowth of the
Centennial Exhibition, now the Philadelphia College
of Art, long may it live!

.

The Liberation of
Clementine Tipton

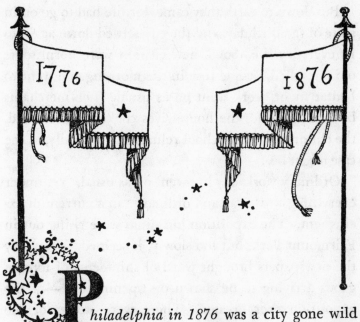

Philadelphia in 1876 was a city gone wild with excitement and jubilation. The New Year's celebration that year surpassed any in the city's history, a blaze of torches and flares and gas jets and Roman candles. The church bells and factory whistles of the entire town joined in the celebration of the country's one hundredth birthday.

Thousands of Philadelphians jammed the streets and the squares, shouting and laughing and singing, not the least discouraged by the rain overhead and the mud underfoot. It was a glorious affair, and it was hard to come down to earth and wait for summer and the opening of the great International Centennial Exposition.

1

But down to earth they came, for life had to go on in spite of the birthday, and the city settled down again to its everyday life. Some new citizens were born, some old ones died, people rose in the morning and went to bed at night, work went on as usual. The merchants bought and sold, the housewives cooked and cleaned, the children went to school reluctantly or gladly, as the case might be.

Ordinary workaday life went on as usual. Yet under everything workaday and ordinary ran a current of excitement. The exposition buildings were rising out in Fairmount Park, but too slowly, it seemed. Every day the newspapers brought word of shipments of foreign goods arriving to be shown on opening day — if the exposition ever opened. There were stories of the behind-the-scenes disagreements and feuding between the various committees, and of money running out all too soon. There were those who were sure that the exposition would never go on, and others who insisted it must.

Philadelphia in 1876 was an interesting place to be.

Chapter One

lementine hitched forward as soundlessly as she could. The last thing she wanted to do was to attract attention to herself, squatting behind the tapestry screen in the morning room. She could hear fine, every word that was being said, but Mama's back blocked completely her view of the woman who would probably be her new governess. She was determined to see and to make up her mind beforehand what the new one would be like.

Actually, even if she turned out to be another horror, Clementine knew she wouldn't have anything to say about it. She had thrown a fit and sassed the last candidate; however, the woman was so outraged that she decided not to accept the position. Clementine was punished, of course, but it was well worth it. That one would have been as bad as Mademoiselle, and Clementine had had five years of that stern and pinch-nosed rule. It was bad enough to be scolded constantly in English, but in French it became almost unbearable. Thank goodness Mademoiselle's mother had fallen ill and her daughter had gone back to France to take care of her. There was a chance, but it was only a chance, that the new governess would be an improvement.

Clementine had run wild for over a month, with no one to supervise her but Nanny, and Nanny already had enough to do taking care of the two little ones. Mama looked distressed when Clementine dashed around with her gloves unmended and her striped stockings wrinkled and her French verbs only half-remembered. At best, Clementine was likely to be distressing, and with the governess gone, Mama was in despair.

This morning had been the last straw. Mama had been so hopeful of getting the Godfreys' French governess, now that the Godfrey children were growing up. And then this morning the postman brought a letter from her, saying that since the Tiptons were planning to remain in Philadelphia for the whole summer, and not go to the seashore as usual, the governess had regretfully decided that she would undertake the care of the Bidwell children and go to Newport for the sea air. Mama disliked Mrs. Bidwell and she was extremely annoyed at being turned down.

"How ridiculous!" she fumed. "Of course we'll be in Philadelphia this summer — with the centennial, and all those distinguished guests coming, and your Papa the chairman of the directors' committee! Well, I'm sure we wouldn't have cared for her anyway, since she's the kind who prefers the Bidwells."

So this Miss Lamb was probably going to be the one,

except that Mama seemed to be hesitating. Clementine wriggled into a more comfortable position and put her eye to the crack in the three-panel screen. She had a perfect view of the back of Mama's lilac morning dress and white lace morning cap and her carefully arranged braids and curls. But the visitor was completely hidden.

Mama was saying, "Your letters of recommendation are excellent, Miss Lamb — a minister's daughter, how nice. Would that be Church of England? But — well, we had planned for someone more mature. You see, although she is only ten, Clementine is — strong-willed, you might say, and difficult, and someone older would be more qualified to guide her, don't you think? You seem so young — "

The new candidate's voice was clear and pleasant, not like Mademoiselle's sharp nasal tones. She said quickly, "Lady Alice felt that I did particularly well with unruly children."

"Oh yes, Lady Alice." Mama glanced again at the letter she held in her hand. "But you are English, and we had hoped for another Frenchwoman. Good French is so important in society these days."

"*Je parle français, Madame Tipton.*"

Clementine drew in her breath. Another one! Oh dear!

"Or perhaps a Scotswoman — they are always so good with children."

" 'Scottish for nannies, English for governesses,'

Lady Alice always said," answered Miss Lamb firmly.

"Oh yes, indeed, Lady Alice." Mama was plainly impressed with the title. Before she could continue there was a tap at the door and Simpson, the butler, entered. What his message was, Clementine couldn't hear, but it evidently required Mama's immediate attention, for she excused herself, saying, "So tiresome, these household details. Pray make yourself comfortable. I shall return in just a moment."

The instant the door was closed Clementine put her eye to the crack again and this time she could see perfectly. Miss Lamb sat bolt upright on her straight chair, her back as stiff as a ramrod. She darted quick glances around the room, looking at the heavy damask draperies that were looped back at the windows, the walls hung with gold-framed paintings, at the carved chairs, the gold and white and black marble fireplace, the ferns on their tables, the writing desk where Mama answered her mail — this Miss Lamb didn't miss a thing.

Her voice sounded all right, very English, much like that of Simpson, the butler. But it was hard to tell about her looks. She was small and almost, though not quite, pretty. She had smooth brown hair drawn back into a knot, pink cheeks, and bright brown eyes. She wore a neat dark blue dress and coat and a bonnet that managed to be both businesslike and becoming. Here Clementine hitched closer to the crack to see better, and the screen wobbled. She grabbed it before it fell, but the bright brown eyes had noticed the slight motion. In a flash Miss Lamb was across the room. Clementine looked up from her crouched position to find Miss Lamb looking down at her.

"Is this the difficult Clementine? Eavesdropping?" Miss Lamb wanted to know, sternly. Clementine nodded and stood up, smoothing her rumpled pinafore.

"I just wanted to check," she said defiantly. "I wanted to see what you'd be like. After all, if I've got to live with you — "

"You might say the same for me, you know. If I've got to put up with you day and night, I'd like to know what kind of person you are. Sit down and tell me."

Well, this was a change! Mademoiselle had never given a hoot what Clementine was or wanted to be. It was always what Mademoiselle thought she should be.

"I'm — well, Mama says I'm a problem." Better let her know right away. "I yell and stamp."

"Oh?"

"And once I bit Mademoiselle. Only once. But she deserved it."

"Do you often act like that?" Miss Lamb didn't seem particularly shocked, just interested.

"Oh no, only when I just can't stand it anymore. 'Do this! Do that! Don't be so clumsy, don't be stupid, don't be so awkward, mind your manners, fix that dreadful hair, remember your curtsy, lower your voice, conjugate your verbs, pull up your stockings, don't

lose your gloves!' And all in French. It sounds worse in French," she added gloomily. "If I lived to be a hundred I'd never be able to please Mademoiselle."

"That's odd. I'm rather pleased with you already."

Clementine looked hard at her, trying to see if she could be telling the truth. It was difficult to tell. She had a crisp, brisk, no-nonsense way of talking that sounded severe, but then she had talked to Mama the same way. Mademoiselle had smirked and spoken sweetly in front of Mama and Papa, and then pulled Clementine's ear or rapped her knuckles when they were alone.

"You're pleased? Really?"

"Really. Because I like a bit of spirit in a child, and you've plenty of that, it seems."

"Then keep talking about Lady Alice. Mama just loves lords and ladies and dukes and duchesses."

There was no time for more conversation. Mama's heels clicked down the hall and the morning-room door opened.

"Please forgive me, my dear; so many things to attend to — Why, I see you've met Clementine."

Miss Lamb and Clementine both curtsied.

"We've been getting acquainted, Mama. Miss Lamb is very nice. Can I take her upstairs now and show her the schoolroom?"

"*May* I, Clementine," Mama corrected automatically. "Oh, dear, we really hadn't settled anything."

Mama plainly felt she was being rushed. "Miss Lamb and I should discuss this further —"

Clementine wanted to get the matter settled.

"She'll do just fine, Mama, I'm sure of it." This wasn't the best possible recommendation in Mama's eyes. Clementine had one of her sudden inspirations.

"I'm to learn embroidery, and keep my stockings straight at all times. Lady Alice insisted on things like that."

Mama missed Miss Lamb's startled look, but Clementine caught it. *Lady* was a magic word for Mama, and she struggled only a moment before she gave in.

"Of course, if Lady Alice insisted — You see what I mean, Miss Lamb? Clementine is such a hard-headed child, so willful. You must be very firm, and well — It's for a trial period, of course, just to see if it is satisfactory all around —"

"Of course, madam. We must all be happy with the arrangement or I shouldn't care to stay."

"Oh, but you must!" The thought of Clementine governessless again seemed to chill Mrs. Tipton's bones. She shivered. "I'm quite worn out with taking her out with me; she objects so to making calls. Somehow you will have to find a way to curb that streak of wildness. It's so unsuitable for a child of her position. She seems to be bursting out of everything — gloves, conversation, stockings, manners —" Mrs. Tipton shivered again. She lowered her voice and said, "Clementine is unmanageable."

"I certainly will do my best, madam. I don't doubt at all that I will be able to effect great improvements."

Mama appeared relieved at Miss Lamb's firm approach. Clementine said impatiently,

"Well, then if it's all settled, may I show Miss Lamb around?"

"Clementine dear, you're so impatient, so impulsive! It's not mannerly. I trust Miss Lamb will be able to change that. Goodness knows Mademoiselle tried. Shall you be able to begin soon?"

"Today, madam, if you like."

"Oh, I do like. The sooner the better. Have your things brought round at once and get settled in. Mr. Tipton will speak to you later about schedules and — salary — " Mama hesitated. It wasn't ladylike to speak about money, and Mama always found it difficult.

Miss Lamb answered, "A firm schedule is most necessary. For lessons and exercise as well. I hope you feel strongly about exercise in the fresh air."

Mama agreed eagerly. She believed in fresh air for children and nannies and governesses, but she herself detested fresh air. Miss Lamb evidently was going to be a treasure.

"Then I'll have my things sent round from my lodgings."

Clementine was beginning to wonder. Had she been too quick to decide that she was going to like her new governess? All this talk of improvements and schedules. She sighed. Whatever happened, she

11

hadn't much choice. If it were not Miss Lamb it would be someone else and Miss Lamb seemed to be a notch better than Mademoiselle. More than just a notch, really; a lot more. She took Miss Lamb's outstretched hand obediently; they curtsied and left the morning room together.

"What would you like to see first? The schoolroom, I s'pose."

"First I'll pop round to my lodgings and see to my belongings, and be back this afternoon. I'll inspect the schoolroom then."

Clementine watched her leave. Through the lace curtains of the front parlor she could see Miss Lamb go down the front steps. On the sidewalk, the new governess turned and gave the entire Tipton house a long searching look. She smiled confidently and made a little motion as if she were saluting. Then she went on down the street.

"I wonder what she meant by that?" Clementine asked herself. But she had no answer.

As soon as Miss Lamb was out of sight Clementine hurried downstairs to the big basement kitchen. In the month since Mademoiselle had left, Clementine had discovered a whole new world right under her own roof. Mama and Papa didn't even dream it existed.

The maids who said, "Yes, mum. No, mum. Very good, mum," who moved quietly about the drawing room like expressionless clockwork figures with feather dusters, wearing crisp blue and white stripes in the morning, gray poplin in the afternoon, and black with white lace aprons for evening — these subdued females were quite different creatures once they went down the backstairs. They became alive again, with mussed caps and tumbled hair and hearty Irish laughs.

Mama and Papa would have been surprised to learn that Simpson, the butler, was a real man whose first name was Alfie, although only Cook dared call him that to his face. His feet in his highly polished boots often hurt and he got weary of climbing the stairs in answer to the tinkling of the everlasting bells.

And Cook! Oh, the singing and the complaining and the yelling that Mrs. Culligan did! And the battles with Simpson that never ended in victory for either one! They battled constantly for power, but united when necessary for or against the others. They liked Nanny, for instance, and saw to it that the nursery teas were special. But they had heartily disliked Mademoiselle and sent her up cold muffins for tea whenever they could get away with it.

Between them, Cook and Simpson knew everything that went on in the house — everything! And they discussed it freely. Simpson had already made up his mind about the new governess.

"A fine proper-looking young woman," he decided. "Being English, she's without a doubt a great improvement over our late lamented Mademoiselle."

"The divil himself'd be a great improvement over

that one," said Mrs. Culligan bitterly. "But another John Bull about the place, heaven forbid! Haven't we enough troubles on this side of the ocean without bringin' in more of them uppity Britishers? Nose in the air, I'm thinkin', wasn't she, Clem darlin'? And thinkin' herself the one, I'll be bound."

"I don't think so, but it's too soon to be sure," said Clementine. "I'll let you know."

"Out of me kitchen!" roared Mrs. Culligan, slapping at her hand. It was too late. The jam tart disappeared, and Clementine grinned, her mouth too full to talk.

"Yer dinner'll be spoiled, and serves you right. The tarts are special ordered, and there'll be only enough — "

Clementine left the kitchen before Mrs. Culligan could say anything more, and escaped up the backstairs to the third floor and Nanny.

Nanny McGregor was Scottish, stout and red-faced and loving. She had had the care of Clementine until she was five, and then Mademoiselle had taken over. She did her best to look after Clementine after Mademoiselle left, but the little ones, Titus and Baby Adelaide, kept her busy. They were the center of her world now as Clementine once had been. She managed to hear Clementine's prayers at night and brush the bright brown hair that curled so stubbornly, and occasionally oversaw her choice of clothes.

For the rest of the day Clementine ran wild. When

her mother thought of it, she was told to bring her French reader and her copybook to the sitting room, and together they struggled through the lesson. But it was exhausting and exasperating for Mrs. Tipton and even worse for Clementine. Most of the time Clementine was clever enough to stay out of sight down in the kitchen, where currents of excitement and contention and drama swirled all day long. She polished silver and peeled potatoes, and her mother wondered why her hands were so rough and red and unladylike.

She breathed in the family stories and the gossip and the rich smells of roasts and gravies and bacon frying. Now with the hiring of Miss Lamb this lovely backstairs life would have to end. Clementine would be returned forcibly to the pale, refined world of Mama's teas in the drawing room, with polite murmuring ladies. And making calls, perhaps, and sedate walks in the park. There would be those lessons again, and scoldings for things done and undone, and clean white gloves and unwrinkled stockings.

There was only a chance that life with Miss Lamb would be better than life with Mademoiselle, and that chance was a small one. Well, she would put up a fight as long as she could, but in the long run, Clementine knew, parents and governesses always came out ahead.

Then she thought about the smile and the little wave that Miss Lamb had given the Tipton house. She didn't know what it signified exactly, but for some reason she felt hopeful.

Chapter Two

he 2200 block on Spruce Street was a fine one. The large houses, brick and brownstone and marble, had stood close together for a long time. Trees cast their long shadows over the red brick sidewalks. The spotless white marble steps led up to huge dignified front doors. The long windows were draped with velvet, and lace curtains blocked the view inside. But though these handsome houses stood close together, each was a completely separate world. The inhabitants bowed politely and distantly if they chanced to meet, but there was no neighborly calling back and forth or back-fence gossip. Each house kept strictly to itself.

The Tipton house on the corner was a complicated, fascinating kingdom. It was only since Mademoiselle had left that Clementine had discovered what a complicated place it really was. Besides Mr. Horace Tipton and his wife there were the three children and Nanny, their nurse, and now there would be a governess again to teach Clementine her lessons and her manners. Then there was a whole crew of others who kept the house going from early morning until late at night.

Clementine had been born there, in the big master bedroom at the top of the stairs. It was the only house she had ever known, except for seaside cottages which didn't count, and she knew every inch of it. If she had been blindfolded, she would have known exactly where she was just by the smells.

There were the rich strong warm smells of the kitchen, of bread rising and baking. In the drawing room there were the delicate elegant smells of the lemon oil on the shining floors, the vases of flowers that Mama arranged every morning. There was a pot-pourri of rose petals and spices in a Chinese jar on the mantel. The conservatory where old Lowndes puttered and pruned his precious flowers smelled of warm earth and orange trees. The library had its own musty aroma of good cigars and leather-covered books that were often dusted but seldom read.

The second floor bedrooms — the big one for Mama and Papa and all the rest for guests — smelled cool and fresh, and the fragrance was sharpened when the doors to the linen closet were opened. Lavender sachets were tucked between the stacks of sheets. And Mama's dressing room was sweet with rose water and lilac cologne and French perfumes.

Clementine's bedroom on the third floor held a mixture of smells — apples she had filched from the kitchen getting punky on the window sill, the dusty smell of baby talc and the faintly sour baby smell that came from the nursery across the hall. And at the back of the third floor — chalk dust. You couldn't miss the schoolroom smell.

The fourth floor's smell was starch — starched petticoats, starched caps, starched aprons so stiff they could stand by themselves. The clean laundry smell overrode Sheila's eau de Paris and the camphor and mutton-tallow mixture Katie Rose rubbed on her feet in winter.

A house so large had to be run on a strict timetable. Always the first to be up and around was Mrs. Culligan, the cook, in her little bedroom off the kitchen: she woke reluctantly.

"Glory be to God," she muttered. "It's time already." Still dazed with sleep, she groped for her old flannel wrapper. She thrust her arms into the sleeves, and without bothering to button it, she clutched it around her ample body and staggered out into the kitchen.

It was like a great dark cave in the basement of the house, the fire in the cookstove only a dull red glow. With a clatter and a rattle she shook down the ashes and poked the fire up to a leaping flame and added a pail of coal. She lit the oil lamp so that it shed a bright circle of light over the big empty table. The kettles had been filled the night before and set on the back of the stove, and the water was almost warm enough already. In a short time the smallest kettle came to a

boil and Cook poured the water into a teapot. She set it on the table with a bang. She made no effort to be quiet; in fact, she made as much noise as she could.

"The lazy good-for-nothin'," she said, thinking of Simpson. "The cheek of him, a-layin' abed at this hour of the mornin', whilst others slave and struggle for him so's he can have his cup of English tea. Irish tea's not good enough for him, of course." Grumbling aloud, she tied a big apron over her wrapper and rolled up her sleeves.

As if in answer to her banging and muttering, Simpson came down the stairs from his room on the fourth floor. Tall, thin, with only a suggestion of a pot belly, he was always as well groomed as Mrs. Culligan was slovenly, even though it was still so early. He was completely dressed, except for his tailcoat, which he put carefully over the back of his chair.

"Good morning, Mrs. Culligan. You're looking as lovely as ever, my dear, which is not saying much."

"None of that, you evil old goat!" She poured his tea, splashing it over into the saucer. He winced, and then drank it gratefully. She sat down at her end of the table, propping her head in her hand, and drank her strong Irish tea noisily. And after that they both were more cheerful.

Mrs. Culligan started breakfast and Simpson began his preparations for the day. He pulled the bell cord that rang a bell way up on the fourth floor where the maids were sleeping, and then got ready the covered silver dishes and platters he had brought down to the kitchen the night before. When Mrs. Culligan had filled them, the platters would all go back up again to the morning room where Mr. and Mrs. Tipton would breakfast. Simpson set the table there at his leisure since it was still early, but with an eye on the clock, nevertheless. Mr. Tipton did not like to be kept waiting.

Simpson was part way up the backstairs when Katie Rose came flying down. "G'mornin', Mr. Simpson. Am I late?"

Without waiting for an answer she raced on, and behind her clattered the rest of the girls — Kathleen and Mary Catherine and Sheila and Rosemary, caps askew, tying on their frilled aprons as they ran. Later on, each one would have her duties in her own special part of the house, but in the early morning they all helped with everything.

Breakfast was a substantial meal in the Tipton household for family and help alike. Mr. Tipton was demanding, but he was not stingy, and unlike some other grand houses in the neighborhood, the servants here were as well fed belowstairs as their master and mistress above.

By now Mrs. Culligan had prepared platters of chops and ham, fried to perfection. Potatoes were browning in the skillet, piles of toast had been browned over the fire and kept hot in the oven. Usually there was hot kippered herring in case Mr. Tipton cared for a bit of fish as well. Mrs. Culligan had the eggs warmed to room temperature, waiting for a signal from Simpson. When Mr. Tipton cracked open his boiled eggs he expected to find them cooked four minutes exactly, no more, no less.

Everything was ready, waiting to be loaded on the dumbwaiter and hauled upstairs as soon as they heard the tinkle of the bell that said Mr. Tipton was ready. It was all like a well-planned play, with the actors waiting for the signal to begin as the curtain goes up.

Simpson went quietly up the stairs in his felt slippers and knocked on the door of the master bedroom. He knew that no one would notice his slippers so early in the morning. Later on would be soon enough to put his aching feet into stiff shoes. He drew open the heavy draperies, touched a match to the wood in the fireplace, and said in just the right tone of voice, neither too cheerful nor too grim, "Good morning, sir and madam."

In the meantime Katie Rose had lighted in the fire in Mrs. Tipton's dressing room. The hot water was steaming in the wash bowl, a morning gown was laid out for her mistress and Katie tiptoed out. She stayed within call in case she was needed to tighten the strings of Mrs. Tipton's corsets.

When Mr. Tipton was ready to start down the front stairs he pulled the bell cord by the bed. The bell tinkled in the kitchen, the ropes of the dumbwaiter creaked, breakfast rose slowly from the kitchen to the morning room. By the time Mr. Tipton reached the morning room, Simpson was ready for him: the newspaper was folded by his plate, his coffee poured.

The morning schedule was the same every day, neither late nor early by so much as a minute. Mr. Tipton checked the time with his gold pocket watch, nodded, and began to eat.

Mrs. Tipton was not nearly so punctual, although she tried hard. She knew her husband liked her to be on time, but it took her longer to dress and arrange her hair. Her husband had eaten his way through ham and eggs and potatoes and toast and herring and a lamb chop and was on his second cup of coffee when she glided in and took her place at the table.

Up on the third floor, Clementine had been dawdling through her dressing, but when the bell tinkled again she quickly buttoned her fresh pinafore and hurried out. She clumped down the first flight of stairs but remembered in time to walk quietly like a little lady. Before Mademoiselle had left, Clementine had had breakfast in the nursery, but for now she was allowed to breakfast with her parents. Her father saw her only at breakfast and for a few minutes at tea time, so it was important that she try to behave. She winked at Simpson and when he had a chance he winked back. Clementine had a hearty appetite so he filled her plate, but Mrs. Tipton had only tea and toast. She was tall and pretty and slender and intended to remain that way, and besides, her tightly laced corsets did not let her eat much.

Breakfast of oatmeal porridge and scones and hot milk had already gone up to Nanny and the children in the nursery. Nanny watched the clock, too, and hurried Titus with his porridge. Titus was three, and poky, and it was hard to get him and Baby Adelaide dressed and fed at exactly the right time. Just before Mr. Tipton finished his coffee each morning, Nanny came hurrying in, carrying Adelaide and leading Titus by the hand. Mr. Tipton put Titus on his knee and gave him toast and jam. Adelaide blew kisses to them all from her mother's lap. Adelaide was a good baby and Nanny could count on her to be happy and laughing. She was not always so sure about Titus and Clementine.

Then it was time for Mr. Tipton to leave to Go To Business. Pat, the coachman, had gulped part of his breakfast in the kitchen and now had the carriage waiting outside. He would be back for another breakfast later. From morning until night the fire would be burning brightly in the cookstove. The teakettle never cooled off, and someone was always having just a bite of whatever Mrs. Culligan was making. Mrs. Pat could take her time about eating before she went back to straighten the rooms over the carriage house where she and Pat lived. Later she would be back in the kitchen to gossip as she rocked and did the mending, baskets and baskets of it. Mr. and Mrs. Tipton might think the household was run from the drawing room or the desk in the library where the accounts were kept, but the kitchen was the heart of the house, whether they knew it or not.

When Simpson had helped Mr. Tipton into his greatcoat, handed him his hat and cane and held the front door open, when Pat had driven away, the house on the corner of Spruce Street seemed to heave a great sigh. There was plenty to do the rest of the day, but the schedule would be more relaxed. A minute or two more or less would not matter so much.

Mrs. Tipton lingered on at her writing table in the morning room while Simpson cleared away the dishes. She read the mail, wrote answers to the many invitations, sent out scented notes written with her gold-tipped pen.

Mrs. Culligan, combed and brushed and neat now in her blue and white striped uniform and spotless white apron, came upstairs to discuss the meals for the day. There used to be a housekeeper, a stern and efficient New England woman named Hyde, who planned the meals and the marketing with Mrs. Tipton and then passed the orders on to Cook. But Cook hated Hyde and refused to take her orders, and when Mrs. Tipton was forced to choose between them, she had to choose Cook. Because whatever else her failings, and Mrs. Tipton had no idea how many failings Mrs. Culligan really had, she cooked like an angel.

Even Simpson had to admit that. Mrs. Tipton's dinner parties were the talk of society, and Mrs. Culligan could never be replaced.

If Mrs. Culligan was queen of the house, then surely Simpson deserved to be called king. (And it would not be the first time that a king and a queen couldn't stand one another.) Mrs. Culligan prepared delicious food, but it was Simpson who saw that it was served with style, that the house was shining and spotless, that the backstairs quarrels and rivalries stayed there and never intruded into the parlor. He planned the duties of each of the maids and made sure that everything was done right. It was twice as much work for him when Hyde went away, but it was clear that Mrs. Tipton had made the right choice, as Simpson remarked appreciatively whenever he enjoyed Cook's apple pie.

No sooner was breakfast out of the way than the street cries were heard from the alley behind the carriage house and stable. The milkman clanged his bell and Kathleen and Sheila ran out to the wagon with their containers for milk and cream and country butter. When his horse clip-clopped away, the butcher's cart pulled up. The butcher had a voice like a bull: "me-e-at, meat, fine fresh beef and pork and what you will!" Mrs. Culligan hurried out to argue with him over the cuts of meat and the prices, for she claimed she could not trust him farther than she could throw a soup bone.

When the vegetable vendors came with their pushcarts and baskets, Mrs. Culligan was out there again, with a shawl thrown over her shoulders, selecting every apple personally, thumping the winter squashes, hefting the cabbages. She shouted at the Italian vegetable man and he shouted back. He could not understand her thick Irish brogue, she could not understand his broken English. So they both shouted to make themselves understood.

All day long the house on Spruce Street echoed with interesting sounds, from indoors and out. Heels clicked on the stairs and in the halls, Pat and the carriage came and went, taking Mrs. Tipton shopping and making calls. The horses stamped and whinnied at the hitching post in front of the house, and stamped and whinnied in the stable. The nursery was noisy with Adelaide's laughing and sometimes with her crying, and with Titus's crashing building blocks and trains.

Lunch and tea trays and suppers were carried up and down the backstairs. The teakettles sang in the kitchen and on the schoolroom stove. If Mr. and Mrs. Tipton were entertaining, the sounds of the house were polite and genteel. The front doorbell rang, the door opened and closed, there was quiet talking and restrained laughter in the parlors and the dining room. The ladies looked beautiful, like something out of a fairy tale, in satins and ruffles and jewels.

Later there would be music in the drawing room. Perhaps a singer might come to perform, or a harpist

27

would play a gentle tinkling concert. Some of the guests talked right on through the music and never heard a note of it, but when the music was over they applauded, clapping discreetly, saying, "Divine, lovely voice, superb repertoire." Then murmuring, "My dear, it has been such a delightful evening — enjoyed it immensely, Tipton, Olympia darling — we'll lunch together soon, promise you won't forget — so really elegant, so very pleasant," the guests left. Their carriages bore them away into the winter darkness, and Mr. and Mrs. Tipton yawned and went up to bed.

In the kitchen there was still some activity, but not the hustle and bustle of the morning. The great piles of dishes from dinner were washed and dried and stacked on the dumbwaiter to be hauled up in the morning.

Mrs. Pat usually popped in for one more visit and a last cup of tea. Pat had already retired. He knew he would be needed early the next morning. Mrs. Culligan soaked her feet, peeling potatoes for breakfast and lecturing the maids all at the same time. They drank their tea and paid no attention to Cook at all. Tomorrow Mary Catherine would have a night off and her beau would be calling for her. She and Kathleen talked about clothes and Kathleen offered to lend her some gloves. Katie Rose rubbed her aching legs and swore softly to herself. Rosemary wrote a little on a long letter to her mother and found it hard going. She did not write very well, but then her mother did not read very well so it all came out all right.

Once in a while a carriage rolled by and faintly they heard the sound of horses' hooves. The city and the street and the big house were almost quiet. Spruce Street was settling down for the night.

Chapter Three

he porter, directed excitedly by Clementine and calmly by Simpson, stumped up the stairs to the third floor, put down Miss Lamb's small steamer trunk, and left with his tip. Clementine asked, "Well, is it all right?"

Miss Lamb looked around the small room that was to be hers. It was even smaller than Clementine's bedroom next door, but there was a wardrobe for her clothes, a shelf for her books and a lamp and a mirror — she had an idea that appearance was important in the Tipton household — and a bed. And that was it.

"Very nice," she said to Clementine. "It'll do just fine." When her clothes were hung in the wardrobe and her books placed carefully on the shelf, they went into the schoolroom. Again, a very quick examination was enough. It was a big bare room at the back of the house. It was brightened by the morning sunshine but shadowed now in the late afternoon. A generous fire was crackling in the stove. Simpson had seen to that.

Clementine had always hated the room and she was prepared to go on hating it. There sat her desk, and a

larger one for the governess, with a globe and the ruler
for rapping knuckles. Miss Lamb looked it over and
smiled.

"A beautiful room for learning," she said enthusiastically. "We'll begin tomorrow. For today, let's sit
here by the fire and go over your books and get acquainted."

Clementine was glad to postpone learning as long as
possible, and she hurried to get her reader and her

French grammar and the copybooks that were so hard to keep neat.

They settled down by the fire. At first Clementine sat very still and straight as Mademoiselle had always insisted, but after a few minutes of silence she began to fidget. It was too quiet with only the sound of pages turning and the coal snapping in the grate.

Miss Lamb made occasional notes and finally said, "Well, now, that's not a bad plan. Suppose we study in the morning and after dinner another lesson, then out-of-doors, weather permitting, with French conversation as we walk, and then some fine sewing or perhaps painting — oh, that reminds me. May I see your sewing? And tell me, please, about Lady Alice and her fondness for embroidery and neat stockings." Miss Lamb's tone was stern, yet underneath she seemed to be laughing.

Well, the ruler and the knuckle-rapping had to come sooner or later, Clementine thought. She put her hands behind her back and tried to think how she could best carry it off.

"I made that up about Lady Alice," she said airily. "I thought it would help Mama to decide quicker."

"Oh, you made it up? Just like that, without a shred of truth to it? A bold-faced lie?"

"I didn't intend to lie — not exactly. It just popped out when I opened my mouth." The off-hand approach wasn't working with Miss Lamb.

"We'll have no more of that!" the governess said

firmly. "I won't stand for untruthfulness, do you understand?" Clementine nodded, shamefaced.

Miss Lamb had pressed her lips together in a tight disapproving line, and then the corners of those lips twitched. She was trying not to laugh! A giggle escaped in spite of her attempt to be serious.

"Oh, Clementine! Lady Alice and neat stockings! If only you knew! Lady Alice wouldn't notice a wrinkled stocking unless it fell down altogether and then only if it interfered with mounting her horse. And embroidery! She wouldn't have an idea which end of the needle to thread."

Clementine was enormously cheered by this news until Miss Lamb added, "Of course that doesn't mean you may wear baggy stockings, Clementine. And we will have embroidery lessons, since you told your mother we would, but we won't hold Lady Alice responsible."

"What — what will the other lessons be?" She was almost afraid to ask.

"All the usual things — spelling and grammar and arithmetic and French, geography and history. I thought we might pay special attention to history since this is your hundredth birthday year here in America."

"You know about the centennial? Even in England, did you hear about it?"

"England's not that far from the center of things, Mistress Know-it-all," said Miss Lamb. She seemed a bit miffed. "We have newspapers, you know, and news gets around. In fact, the centennial is what brought me here, that and Her Ladyship's black bull."

She laughed as if she was remembering something very funny, but before Clementine could ask any more questions there was a knock on the schoolroom door.

It was Sheila with the tea tray. There was a bustle of clearing off the table to make room, and of introducing Miss Lamb to the youngest and newest of the Tipton housemaids. Sheila was fresh from County Cork, still clumsy with the dishes and apt to drop things, but Simpson was training her and soon she would be trusted to serve at dinner. She was acting very haughty and cool, in spite of her curiosity about the new governess, for she did not intend to give Miss Lamb a chance to snub her as Mademoiselle had always done. Mademoiselle had not been liked by the rest of the help. She had been sharp-tongued and demanding of her rights, and scornful of the Irish maids whom she considered far beneath her. So Sheila was prepared for the worst.

Instead Miss Lamb smiled warmly, shook Sheila's hand, and thanked her for the tray.

"A cup of tea is just what I've been longing for," she said gratefully. "I wasn't sure it was the custom in America." The ice on Sheila's brogue quickly melted.

"Oh, indade, and if you'll ever be wantin' a cup at odd hours, the kittle's always at the boil down in the kitchen. You've only to stop by."

Sheila would carry a good report back to the

34

kitchen. She was carrying a message from Mrs. Tipton, too.

"Your mama'll not be up to say good night this evenin', for she's goin' to take tea at the Blackstones', and himself'll be meetin' her there and goin' on to a dinner party and centennial meeting. You are to have tea and supper combined, so Cook's made it a good one, and the madam'll see you both after breakfast tomorrow."

Mrs. Culligan had made it a good one. When Clementine spooned out the last of her cup custard and finished off the rest of the buncake, she leaned back in her chair and sighed happily.

"Just think," she said. "Harriet and Margery Blackstone are all dressed up this very minute, handing out the teacups for their mother, and curtsying to my mama and all the rest of the ladies. And I'm here, free as a bird."

"You don't care for teas, then?"

"I like the food," she said honestly. "But I do despise the talking and the dressing up. I don't see how Mama does it day after day, and never says the wrong thing. Every word I say turns out to be not polite, even when I don't mean it that way. And I slop tea into the saucers when I pass the cups, and Mama is humiliated. I guess Mama is humiliated every time she makes me go out with her."

Miss Lamb added a quick note to her list. "Practice pouring tea and passing," she murmured. At Clementine's indignant glance she said, "See here, I think it's rather a bore myself, but if it is part of your way of life you may as well learn to do it nicely and easily. Everyone has a few things she hates to do and has to learn anyway. Learn them and get it over with and then go on to the more interesting things."

Before the list could get any longer Clementine suggested that they go downstairs and meet the rest of the help "all in a bunch. That way you'll know everybody and you won't feel strange here."

So they went down the backstairs to the kitchen in the basement of the house. Miss Lamb seemed very confident and assured, not at all timid, but Clementine noticed that she patted the skirt of her navy blue governess dress into place, and made sure the lace at the neckline fell in neat folds.

Clementine pushed open the door and rushed in, sure of her welcome, and Miss Lamb followed.

"Here she is!" Clementine announced. "Here's my new teacher, and she's Miss Lamb, right fresh from England."

Simpson rose to shake her hand cordially and make her welcome. Mrs. Culligan, her feet in a tub of hot water, waved her hand grandly.

"Do come in, me dear, and have a cup of tea with us." Sheila must have carried a very good report for Mrs. Culligan to be so friendly to a new arrival. In a moment Miss Lamb had been introduced all around to the group of young Irish maids and to Pat and Mrs. Pat. Pat was waiting up until it would be time to get the horses out for one more trip, this time to bring the Tiptons home. Then the horses would have to be rubbed down and blanketed, and the carriage given a quick swipe with a rag to remove any spattered mud. The carriage had to be in sparkling condition for the first trip out the next morning. Pat's day was a long one, and he was resting now with his feet propped up on the door of the cookstove.

Mrs. Pat had her usual mending, and she sat with a huge basket in her lap, darning stocking heels with tiny stitches. Simpson and Katie Rose went on with their silver polishing, and Mary Catherine worked on an ornate piece of brass that had grown tarnished. The work in the big house was never really over.

Pat was grumbling, and after all the introductions were over he took up his complaint again. "Meetings, meetings! Three times a week at least himself is out to a meeting about the centennial. Sunday, we're no sooner home from church and grab a bite to eat when we're off again to inspect the grounds and count the new nails as have been pounded in during the past week. For me, anyway, it'll be a great day when the blasted thing is over and done with."

Mrs. Culligan turned on him indignantly. "Sure'n you're the ignoramus, now. The cintinnial is the greatest thing has happened here for a hundred years, and you'll not be around to celebrate the next one, praise be. I'm about to toughen up me feet for walkin' and injoyin' ivery bit of it, so I am."

"The best celebrating I can think of would be to stay at home for once," Pat answered. "What do I care about them foreigners and their buildings, and as for the Women's Pavilion, the less said the better! Like to fall down around their heads, I'll be bound, and serve 'em right!"

Mrs. Culligan was aroused, and she roared, "And why should it fall down, then, tell me that! Why shouldn't us women have a buildin', I'd like to know. Sure we've done enough of the dirty work all our lives. Time we had something to show off to the world!"

Simpson interrupted to ward off the quarrel that was brewing. "And you, Miss Lamb, are you planning to visit the fair and see what our former colony has to show for its first one hundred years?"

"Oh, yes indeed, Mr. Simpson. That was the reason I chose Philadelphia of all the cities here, because of the fair. I quite look forward to it."

Mrs. Culligan lifted one foot from the tub and said, "Water's coolin' off. Pat, you limb of the divil, put in a bit more hot, will you now?"

Without bothering to get up all the way, Pat reached for the kettle and splashed some water over her feet. It was too hot and she answered with a furious bellow.

Miss Lamb rose quickly and attempted to get Clementine out of the kitchen before she had absorbed the full effect of all the profanity. At the same time, she tried to be polite and tactful and excuse their hurry on the lateness of the hour.

Clementine grinned. It was a good try, but it made no difference. She knew all Mrs. Culligan's rich vocabulary by heart, and she planned to repeat it where it would do the most good the first chance she got.

It was bedtime, anyway, so she got ready without an argument. Miss Lamb was tired, too.

"It's been a long day," she yawned. "I'll get to bed myself."

Simpson had explained the series of bells that rang through the third and fourth floors, clanging loudly in the maids' rooms, tinkling softly to remind the governess and nurse that they must get their charges up and presentable for greeting Mr. Tipton at breakfast time. And, said Simpson, the worst mistake you could make was lateness or untidiness, for that would start the master's day off wrong, and that was to be avoided at all costs.

"Well, now you've met us all," said Clementine, "except for Papa, of course, and Grandpa Tipton. He doesn't come so often; just pops in once in a while. He's a funny man."

Of them all, Clementine thought maybe she loved Grandpa best. It was plain that he loved her. He was a very outspoken old man and he made no secret of his feelings. He seemed more amused than shocked when she got herself in trouble, and always defended her.

He ruffled Clementine's springy curls until they stood straight out from her head, and he teased her, and answered all the questions that no one else would ever bother with, such as those about Cook and Simpson.

"Why do they fight all the time? Is it because she's fat and he's thin?"

"Gracious no, nothing so complicated as that. She's Irish and he's English. They feel obliged to carry on the war as a matter of patriotic duty. They're friends, under all the insults."

"Mama says she thinks she made a mistake. If she had it to do over again she'd hire all one kind or the other, so everything would go smoother. Not me — I'd mix 'em all up, all kinds of people."

"Good for you, Clemmy. You're one after my own heart!"

He usually finished up any talk by saying, "Now, let's see what that old curmudgeon Culligan is stirring up for dessert. Could it be an apple pie?"

Miss Lamb heard Clementine's prayers and tucked her into bed. Suddenly Clementine remembered something.

"You never finished telling me about Lady Alice. How did her black bull get you to America?"

Miss Lamb laughed softly. "That's a story for another day. We'll have lots of time to tell each other things."

"Is it a funny story?"

"Funny and frightening and dramatic and ridiculous! We'll save it for a dull day when there's not much to laugh about."

Clementine heard Miss Lamb blow out the lamp, heard her mattress creak a few times, and then it was quiet. It had been a long day, but a nice one. She had a new governess and, it seemed, a new friend. Before she could think any more about it she was fast asleep.

Chapter Four

he next morning Mrs. Tipton was only slightly interested in the program of studies Miss Lamb suggested. She glanced at the list, but her mind was plainly on something else.

"Gracious," she said, "these subjects are so — fierce! You'll make a scholar out of the child!" She laughed lightly, as if nothing more ridiculous than a scholarly child could be imagined. "Penmanship and spelling, of course, and French, naturally. Embroidery, very nice. Painting? Oh, charming. Every well-brought-up girl should have these little accomplishments, don't you think? And since Clementine has so few — She has absolutely resisted piano lessons and disrupted Mrs. Procter's dancing class. I was never so humiliated! As for the rest — history, geography — I don't think we need bother, really."

She gave the list some thought for a moment and then handed it back to the governess.

"We've much more exciting things to think about. Clementine, your Aunt Maude is coming from Pittsburgh sometime soon. She isn't sure just when, but soon." She fluttered a pack of letters. "All these came at once this morning. Maude has been making up her mind for weeks and writing me, and then posted all the letters at once. How like her!"

"Is Aunt Maude coming alone?"

"Goodness, no. She'll bring little Nathaniel and his nurse, of course, and Edwin. The older boys are all away at school. Now I must send word to the dressmaker immediately. She simply must make time for us. And she must bring her niece to help. Maude will want heaps of new things; she always does. Mrs. Pat can let the mending go for a while and lend a hand with seams and hems. Oh, Clementine, won't it be enjoyable, all the teas and parties and dinners and calls? Mercy, how will we ever do it all? And it will be so nice for you to play with your cousin Edwin."

"Ha!" said Clementine bitterly. Miss Lamb's lips twitched, but Mrs. Tipton did not notice and rushed on, "Well, run along, my dears, and do your little studying. Just use your judgment, Miss Lamb, and remember that we want Clementine to be an accomplished young lady, not a dried-up bookworm."

She tried to smooth Clementine's rebellious curls, tied her sash in a neater bow, and dismissed them both with a smile.

It was plain that Miss Lamb was disappointed at Mrs. Tipton's lack of interest in her carefully planned course of study. Clementine agreed with her mother — studies were not her favorite way of spending her day — but she couldn't help feeling a little sorry for Miss Lamb.

They went upstairs to the schoolroom. Clementine sat at her small desk and got out her copybooks and pencils, and then sat waiting for her governess to turn from the sunny window. When Miss Lamb finally sat down at her desk she said earnestly, "There are always more ways than one to accomplish anything worthwhile, Clementine. Remember that. If one door is closed to you, another is sure to open. Now let us begin on spelling, for it is plain that you have much to learn in that area."

The lessons went on quietly. To her surprise, Clementine found she wasn't dreading school hours nearly as much as she used to. When she made a mistake she was told about it gently, with no rapping of knuckles, no impatient outcries, no threats of future punishment.

On the first day Miss Lamb assigned twenty-five words from Clementine's spelling book. By the next day the list had changed to one that Miss Lamb composed. All the words had a common theme — exploration, navigation, colonization. And at the end of the week Miss Lamb said, "You've done very well, Clementine. For a special treat today, you may write a short essay using as many of the words as you can remember. Perhaps something about the beginning of your country. Make a list first and then write the essay." Clementine groaned aloud, and Miss Lamb glanced at her sternly. So she took up her pencil, and with much heavy breathing and erasing, began to write. Miss Lamb was pleased with the result. "A very nice little history and geography lesson," she said. "We'll do more of this kind of spelling."

They went for a long walk each day, a brisk jaunt that left them both pink-cheeked and breathless in the March wind. Each day they ventured in a different direction and explored a new neighborhood, talking about it in French as they went. Miss Lamb's French was not, of course, nearly as fluent as Mademoiselle's had been, and often she had to fumble for a word just as Clementine did. She would laugh a little and then the lesson would go on.

Clementine felt like a visitor being shown her own city, for Mademoiselle's idea of outdoor exercise had been a sedate stroll to Rittenhouse Square and back when the weather was fine. All weather was fine for Miss Lamb — rain or shine or late flurry of snowflakes.

"It's a red-brick town," Miss Lamb exclaimed, and Clementine began to notice, really notice for the first time, what her surroundings were like. She looked at the large sedate houses of brick and marble on Spruce Street. And she saw for the first time the small brick houses, row after row after row of them, on nearby streets where she had never walked before.

Miss Lamb soon discovered the secondhand book stalls far down on Market Street where fascinating books were for sale for very little. Every few days she and Clementine sorted over the treasures and came home with two or three books intended to help with spelling; a book about America before the first settlers arrived, one about the still wild West, and one about the colonies. It was an interesting mixture.

The daily walks opened a whole new world for Clementine, a world where women called back and forth as they swept their sidewalks, where cats dozed in the sun on the front steps, where dogs ran unleashed, where the vegetable peddlers came right to the front door, where girls chalked hopscotch squares on the walk and jumped rope unconcernedly among the passersby. It was very different from the way people did things on Clementine's proper block of Spruce Street.

When they were home again it was comforting to sit in the schoolroom and drink tea — cambric tea for Clementine, made mostly of hot milk, and Miss Lamb's tea strong and bracing. On her second day there Simpson had brought up a teapot and a caddy of English tea. "Enough of that terrible Irish brew that will copperplate your stomach and ruin your disposition forever. It would be your undoing, if you don't mind my saying so."

Aunt Maude's plans had sounded so vague that Clementine had not given her arrival a second thought. So it was a real surprise when she and Miss Lamb arrived home from their walk one afternoon to find the front hallway stacked with trunks and boxes.

Pat and Simpson were bringing more boxes from the hansom cab.

"Take care!" called Aunt Maude excitedly. "Take care not to drop any of them — my bonnets, you know. I couldn't choose so I just brought all of them. Olympia, darling sister Olympia, you look so well, so blooming!"

Mama and her sister were hugging each other. Nanny McGregor was greeting Nanny Ferguson, and looking over Baby Nathaniel to see how he compared to Baby Adelaide. Titus was leaping like a jumping jack with excitement.

There was such noise and confusion that Clementine and Miss Lamb weren't even noticed for a moment. Then the greetings and introductions began all over again. Clementine remembered her curtsy when Miss Lamb nudged her, and then she was enveloped in Aunt Maude's perfumed, ruffled, silken embrace.

"Oh, the sweetheart! You are so lucky, Olympia, *two* little girls! And what dears they are! Is she going to favor you, sister? I do hope so; the women on the Tipton side are so dumpy and homely. You're not going to be dumpy, are you, Clementine? *Do* grow slim and graceful, precious, like your mama!"

Clementine straightened her stocky little shoulders and tried to look as tall and slim and graceful as she could. Somehow Aunt Maude always managed to make her feel clumsy.

She looked around for Edwin, half-glad, half-fearful. Sure enough, he jumped out at her from behind a trunk with a loud *boo!* and laughed at her nervous start.

"Did it again," he gloated. "I always can scare you, old Clemmy. Scary old Clemmy, jellyfish Clemmy," he chanted.

She jabbed him with her elbow, for she was forbidden to slap him, ever, and Edwin let out a scream.

"Do try to be quiet, Edwin dear," said Aunt Maude. "Give a hand with some of these boxes. Take your school books up to your room — is he to have the same room as last time, Olympia darling? — and start to unpack." To her sister she said, "Boys! Dreadful creatures, all of them!" She sounded more proud than sorry.

"School books? Mama, I thought I was to be free of school! How can I study without a tutor?"

"Oh dear, that is a problem! Perhaps Miss Lamb can oversee your work occasionally? Just enough to keep him out of mischief. You needn't trouble yourself with anything difficult like Latin, of course."

Miss Lamb smiled. "I'd be delighted to try, ma'am," she said. "Master Edwin can do his lessons with Clementine."

Edwin made a face behind his mother's back and then grinned as he grabbed an armful of books and three of his mother's hat boxes.

"Come on, Clem. Help me get settled and then

49

we'll plan some tricks. We'll have a whale of a time."

"The tricks will all be on me," she answered gloomily, "and you'll have the whale of a time." But she picked up a small leather chest and trudged up the stairs behind him. Miss Lamb followed, and after them they could hear Aunt Maude say in a voice that was meant to be confidential but carried up the stairwell, "She seems like a well-mannered creature, dear, but so *young!* She's hardly older than Clementine." Miss Lamb flushed but did not turn her head.

Later in the schoolroom, Clementine complained to Miss Lamb, "It's nice to have Aunt Maude visit. She stirs things up a bit, but that Edwin Peabody! I never know whether to be glad or sorry when he comes. He's only ten — only a couple of months older than I am — but he thinks because he's a boy he can order me around. And he does, too." She kicked disconsolately at the rung of her chair.

"Why do you allow him to do it?" Miss Lamb was having a quick cup of tea to warm up from their cold walk.

"Well, he's a boy. That makes him smarter and braver."

Miss Lamb set down her teacup with an annoyed rattle. "Why don't you show him that he's not? You are smart and brave, aren't you?"

"Not very."

"Then you'll have to try to pretend until you really are."

"Why? Why do I have to be smart and brave?"

"It's not such a bad idea. Do you think I'd be here if I weren't a little of both? Do you want to grow up slow-witted and fearful and helpless?"

Clementine shook her head vigorously. She was sure she didn't want that.

"Well, then, there's nothing for it but to outwit young Master Edwin. Fortunately I grew up in a large family with plenty of boys. I may have a few ideas. Give me a chance to get acquainted and we'll see what we can do."

Chapter Five

Aunt Maude's visit did stir things up. There were so many callers, morning and afternoon, that Mrs. Tipton and her sister hardly had time to pay calls in return. They entertained at luncheons and dinners and were, in turn, entertained. There was a constant going and coming of visitors and notes and messengers. Pat and the carriage were ready to go at all hours of the day and night.

Life in the schoolroom and the nursery was not much changed, however. Nanny Ferguson and little Nathaniel settled in quite as if they had always lived there. Edwin groaned and grumbled and complained, but Miss Lamb stood for no nonsense. She set him lessons to learn just as hard as he had at home. It was jollier, though. The extra company and the competition made lessons more fun for Clementine. And when lessons were over she and Edwin played in the nursery with the little ones.

Mademoiselle had frowned on games except for very proper things like carefully dressing and undressing a large pop-eyed French fashion doll. Rocking horses and blocks and trains were only for *les enfants*, she said. But Miss Lamb thought it was kind of the older children to build towns and houses for Titus, and Edwin turned out to be a master tower builder.

On one very rainy afternoon, too wet for even Miss Lamb to go walking, the children all played in the warm cozy day nursery while Miss Lamb and the nannies chatted and sewed buttons on their charges' clothes. Nanny McGregor had been nurse to Mama and Aunt Maude when they were little, and she explained to Nanny Ferguson how it had been in the old days.

"Mr. Titus Tipton, the master's father, was a self-made man, as they say, not a proper Philadelphia gentleman at all. He had a hot temper and a warm laugh and a quick wit and hardly a penny to his name. But when Miss Martha set eyes upon him she would have no other. She was a Bellingham, you know, and I understand there was a lot of talk that she'd married beneath her, but she didn't give a fig. And old Mr. Titus — he was young then, of course — he went on and made a fortune and that fortune made him another fortune, and before long he'd hung a rope of pearls on his wife like you wouldn't believe. Big as the oysters they came out of, they were, and I can speak, for in later days many's the time I helped her dress and fastened them around her neck. That was after young Mr. Tipton — Mr. Horace — was married and brought his bride, my Miss Olympia, here to live. I

was her nurse, and she said she couldn't do without me and I came right along with her as lady's maid, you see.

"Now I'm ahead of my story. By the time Mr. Titus had made all that money, and when his only child, Mr. Horace, was old enough to marry, the society folks had accepted the Tiptons, and you can believe there was no one in society who wasn't looking at Mr. Horace for their daughters. He was considered a wonderful catch.

"Well — " here Nanny took a deep breath and reached for another button — "there were the beautiful Ashby sisters; nurse to them, I was, and maid as they grew older. Miss Maude and Miss Olympia, and they quite set the town on its ears. You wouldn't believe the courting that went on. Every eligible rich handsome young man in Philadelphia had hopes of them. And it was Mr. Peabody who got Maude and Mr. Tipton who won Olympia. There was even a visiting lord and an earl, no less, but neither of them had a chance, poor things. The lord was that bowlegged and the earl's Adam's apple bobbed. Oh, those were the days, I tell you! Dancing and partying and flowers by the wagon load!

"So Mr. Horace and Miss Olympia were married and they moved in here in this beautiful house that Mr. Titus Tipton had bought, until they could build a grander one of their own. And I came with them, as I was Miss Olympia's nurse since childhood and she couldn't do without me. No nurse was needed right away so I was her lady's maid and helped out dear Mrs.

Titus Tipton when she needed me. And then Mrs. Titus died — sudden and surprising."

She reached into her bodice for her handkerchief and blew her nose. Nanny Ferguson clucked sympathetically and waited until she could go on.

"Well, after that nothing was the same for old Mr. Titus. He'd made the money for his Martha, you see, and bought the house for her, and went to the balls and the opera. But with her gone, he had no interest. So one day he declared he was tired of everything, fortune, house, the whole thing, and he gave it away."

"Addled in his head from grief!" exclaimed Nanny Ferguson.

"Addled like a shrewd old fox!" Nanny McGregor was indignant. "No man has or had a clearer mind. He just did what he had a mind to. He turned over the business to Mr. Horace and gave him this house for his own, and the money in the bank, too, and kept back only what he needed. He bought a little house in the country on the river. He sits and fishes and reads and putters in his garden, and nobody would ever guess he had been a rich man in his own right. He swore he'd never wear another stiff collar as long as he lived, and he had me let out the waistband of all his trousers afore he left. And he's happy as a clam. He rarely comes to the city — only once in a while to play with the children and stir up his son, who he claims is too solemn and old before his time and needs to learn to laugh a little. He won't go to dinner parties and when they entertain here he has his supper in the nursery. But he always goes to take a look if Miss Olympia is wearing the pink pearls he bought for his wife. He enjoys having another pretty woman wear them."

"He'd have to go far to find two prettier creatures than Mrs. Tipton and Mrs. Peabody. Pity Clementine here doesn't resemble her mother more. Pure Tipton, she looks like."

"Well, not quite," Nanny McGregor said. "She has her mother's lovely clear skin. But that's her grandfather's firm jaw."

Clementine's "lovely clear skin" was flushed bright pink with annoyance. Why did they always talk right in front of her as if she couldn't hear, or was too dimwitted to understand? It was hard enough to be the homely one in a beautiful family; everyone didn't have to be calling it to her attention. She could see without being told that Titus was a handsome little boy, and Adelaide was as pretty as a picture, and good besides.

Miss Lamb quickly turned the conversation away from Clementine by asking a question about the Peabody home in Pittsburgh, and in a moment Edwin and Clementine were romping with Titus, and the uncomfortable moment was forgotten.

Mr. Tipton enjoyed his sister-in-law's visit, and so did the rest of the household, even though there was twice as much work. But however much Mr. Tipton enjoyed the change, he did not allow his schedule to be altered one bit. As usual after church on Sunday, he announced that they would all go out to the centennial grounds and inspect the work that had been done that week.

"All of us, Horace?" asked his wife.

"Why not? We'll all go; the children too. It will do them good."

"Then the nannies must come, and Miss Lamb, too, to keep an eye on Clementine and Edwin."

It was plain that such a large expedition could not fit into the Tipton carriage, so Mr. Tipton gave orders to Pat to hire another from the livery stable. Edwin said immediately that he would go along, and before anyone could stop her, Clementine dashed after them; she got so few chances to go to a place as exciting as a livery stable. Mama didn't even approve of her going back to their own stable to visit Sprite and Velvet, the Tiptons' horses, although she usually managed it anyway. Mademoiselle had been deathly afraid of horses, and besides, she felt herself to be so far above Pat and Mrs. Pat that she wouldn't consider a visit to the stable or to the living quarters over the carriage house.

Miss Lamb loved horses, and they went every day to feed Sprite and Velvet carrots from the kitchen. Mama didn't know about the visits and Clementine was not about to tell.

Pat was disappointingly quick about his business at the livery stable. He just pointed to the carriage and the horses he wanted and said, "Send the bill to Mr. Horace Tipton."

Clementine and Edwin would have liked to linger but Pat warned, "Hustle, you two. You know himself doesn't like to be kept waiting." So they all climbed into the rented carriage for the short ride home.

Mr. Tipton was to drive his own carriage.

"You will be careful, won't you, Horace dear?" asked Aunt Maude anxiously. "And Pat — he will drive slowly, promise me?"

Mr. Tipton promised and passed the word to Pat that the drive was to be a sedate one so that the ladies and the babies would not be frightened. Pat grumbled to himself, "When do I ever get a chance to drive any way but slow and careful, I'd like to know. Is it a racing driver he thinks I am, now?"

Aunt Maude and Mama and Titus went in the carriage that Papa drove. They sat facing each other in the open carriage, for the sun was warm and there was a feeling of spring in the air. With the ruffles of their church-going gowns blowing, and the plumes on Mama's hat and the flowers on Aunt Maude's, the carriage looked like a bouquet of bright flowers.

The next carriage was more like a tin with sardines packed in it. Miss Lamb and the two nannies with the babies on their laps and Clementine and Edwin rode with Pat. It was a tight squeeze, for both Nanny McGregor and Nanny Ferguson were well-padded and side by side they filled up the seat comfortably. The nannies wore their best uniforms, navy blue coats with side folds, and white veils hanging from their neat bonnets. Miss Lamb was dressed in her best, too — navy blue, of course, for that was what governesses always wore, unless they fancied black. Miss Lamb took up much less room and Edwin and Clementine bounced around so much they needn't have bothered with a seat at all.

It was a lovely April day, a nice change from the blustery March weather. The first young green leaves were beginning to show along the tree-lined streets. It was a beautiful day to be out. They clip-clopped along the red-brick streets, Aunt Maude and Mama bowing left and right to friends who were out for a Sunday drive or stroll. Then they were out of the busy part of town and into the pale greenness of Fairmount Park. The road wound by the river, sparkling in the sunshine. As early in the season as it was with the winter chill not quite out of the air, a number of sailboats were out. And here and there a long graceful rowing shell flashed by, with the oarsman trying for greater speed.

The peace and serenity of the river drive was over when they reached the high plateau where the centennial buildings were going up. There they found confusion everywhere, even though no workmen were busy on Sunday. There were great piles of lumber and pieces of marble and stacks of roof tiles everywhere. And deep rutted tracks where heavily loaded carts had evidently stuck in the churned-up mud many times. The grassy meadow was no more, only a field of mud and lumber and crates and workmen's toolsheds and the skeletons of partly finished buildings. It was a discouraging sight to everyone but Mr. Tipton.

"Goodness gracious, Horace," said Mama as he helped her down from the carriage, "surely they'll never be able to complete this all in time. They've only just begun, and it seems to grow worse rather than better."

"Of course they will finish. They must. Really, most of the buildings are up — look at all those down there. Rest assured, when the fair opens all this will be changed."

"For the better, I trust," remarked Aunt Maude. "It could hardly be changed for the worse."

"Nonsense, my dears. Things look much less organized than they really are. Look over there! Memorial Hall is finished to the last nail. We entertained there for all the directors and distinguished visitors from Washington as long ago as last December. And in that direction — the Main Building is almost done. Watch your step; careful of the rough ground."

The nannies were clucking like hens. "Mind the mud, children! Titus, love, don't fall over this lumber! Clementine, Edwin, no running!"

Miss Lamb said, "Titus, give me your hand! Edwin and Clementine, stay close beside me and behave." They stopped running reluctantly, because when Miss Lamb occasionally snapped out an order, she expected to be obeyed without question.

"It will all be in splendid shape by May, rest assured," said Mr. Tipton confidently. "The railway tracks are completely laid and the station is almost finished. They are working on the boat landings, so visitors can come by water up the river as well. We have a troop of gardeners standing by to plant and mow as soon as the buildings are all finished. Philadelphia will have an exposition to be proud of."

"That's a funny-looking house over there," said Edwin, and Mr. Tipton answered, "The Japanese Building, nephew. The construction is so strange that our American workers couldn't figure it out, so they sent a special crew all the way from Japan to erect it. It will be a marvel to see."

"Dear Horace, I only hope it will all be done in time. It seems a hopeless task."

Mr. Tipton was as proud of the construction as if he had pounded in every nail himself. "Oh, Philadelphia will show the world, never fear! There will be visitors from all over, hundreds and thousands of them, and from the highest degree to the humblest, they will marvel at America's ingenuity and — "

He sounded as if he were launching into one of the many speeches he had made in recent months to raise money for this project that was so close to his heart. Aunt Maude headed him off quickly. "And what is that building over there?" she asked.

"The Women's Pavilion," answered Papa in a disapproving voice. "It's nonsense, the whole business, but the women's committee argued and fussed and carried on and insisted on a building of their own. They went out and raised the money for it, too, so we hadn't much choice. Goodness knows what they'll have to put into it. A whole building full of preserves and knitting, without a doubt!"

Mama and Aunt Maude laughed, and the nannies smiled. But Clementine noticed that Miss Lamb stiffened her back and a pink flush spread over her face. Apparently she didn't think Papa's joke was very funny.

In spite of Papa's confident remarks, it truly was hard to see how these acres of buildings, many of them only partly finished, could ever turn into the most exciting and uplifting exposition ever held. No wonder Papa and his committee of directors had such a time persuading people. Clementine only hoped he was right. It would be terrible if so much work was all for nothing.

Before long Nathaniel and Adelaide began to fuss, and Titus began to pull and strain to get away from Miss Lamb's firm grip. It was time to start home again.

Edwin asked and got Papa's permission to ride up on the seat with Pat, but when Clementine said she'd like to ride up there, too, Papa laughed at her fondly.

"So, Clementine, you want to become a liberated woman and do unmaidenly things like drive horses? Next you will want to vote!"

Edwin climbed to the high seat and gave Clementine a smug smile. It was hard to pretend she didn't mind when she did mind so terribly, but she was determined not to give Edwin the satisfaction of knowing she cared one way or the other. Pat let him help hold the reins and he made a big show of shouting orders to the horses, orders that they completely ignored.

Miss Lamb patted her arm understandingly, but even so, the pleasant day was spoiled and Clementine sulked all the way home. Everyone was let out at the front door and Edwin and Pat rode on to the livery stable to return the rented carriage. When Edwin came back he had a particularly sweet expression on his face.

"He's up to no good," Clementine told Miss Lamb. "Whenever he smiles like that, Edwin Peabody is planning something."

"Oh, I don't think so. You're just being oversensitive, Clementine. I know boys."

She may know boys, thought Clementine, but she doesn't know Edwin. Something is going to happen.

Chapter Six

lementine was right. Edwin had been too good for too long. Sooner or later, he was bound to break out. But when? Clementine watched him closely, not sure what he would do, but positive that whenever he did, she would end up as the butt of the joke.

The brief early April spring was over and it seemed almost as if winter were back again. It rained and rained, and except for a few quick walks, Edwin and Clementine and Miss Lamb were housebound. Miss Lamb did her best to keep them amused with games of anagrams and authors after lessons, but after a while even she ran out of ideas.

Edwin had finished his work early one day and was excused from lessons until Clementine caught up. He spent the morning trailing behind Sheila as she hurried about her Wednesday-morning chores. He was hoping she would stand still long enough for him to tie her apron strings to a chair or a doorknob.

Wednesday morning was always a busy time. All the beds, from the top of the house to the basement, were stripped of their sheets and pillowcases and made up fresh. Edwin watched Sheila make trip after trip to a small closet in the third floor hallway, toss in an armload of sheets, and trot back for another great armload. But when he peered into the closet it was empty. Mystified, he followed her to the second floor. The bedding there was of fine smooth linen with waves of lace edging each sheet and pillowcase, with handsome flowing Ts for Tipton embroidered on every one.

The fancy sheets disappeared into the little closet there just as completely as had the plain ones from the beds of the servants and the children. Sheila nudged him out of her way as he stared into the open door.

"Out of me way, Master Edwin dearie; you're wasting me precious time. I've a-plenty to do today and not a minute to fritter away." She flung another pile through the door and turned away.

"Wait!" he said. He grabbed at her skirt. "Where did the sheets go?"

Sheila had been teased often enough about being fresh from the country so she was glad of a chance to pass the teasing along.

"Oho, you can't be a city boy! It's a great dumb country lad you are, indade! A real bumpkin. Have ye never heard of a laundry chute? They're the latest thing in the city and all the best people are a-havin' of them. Saves many a mile of walkin', they do that."

"A laundry chute?"

"Sure, and it does just that. Shoots the laundry to

the basement in a flash, and on Thursday Mrs. Kelly's boy opens the door, takes it out, and hauls it home for his ma to wash and iron. Now out of me way, darlin', or I'll wrap you in a sheet and shoot you down yourself."

Edwin had the idea he had been waiting for. He grinned broadly at Sheila and went downstairs, leaving her to say to herself, "Mrs. Peabody's the lucky one! That boy's an angel, him with his lovely smile!"

The smiling angel-child hurried to the basement kitchen. As soon as she saw him come in, Mrs. Culligan shouted, "Oh, no, ye don't! Don't lay a hand on me teacakes or I'll — "

"I'm not interested in teacakes," Edwin said loftily. "Where's the laundry chute, Cully? Sheila says there's a door in the kitchen." He began to open cupboard doors.

"If Sheila sent you, it's to get you out of her way, and I'll not have you underfoot here. Not interested in teacakes, I'll bet you're not! Leave my cupboard doors alone, ye spalpeen; the laundry door is over there, the last one. And now, out with you! Next it'll be Clem and then even Master Titus and no peace at all in my kitchen. Out!"

Edwin had seen enough. He opened the narrow laundry chute door and saw the heaps of laundry that only a short time before Sheila had flung from upstairs. He slammed the door, grabbed a teacake and was gone before Cook could do more than threaten.

He tiptoed into the classroom where Clementine was doing sums at her desk. Miss Lamb was busy correcting the long test she had given them, hoping to keep both of her students occupied. Edwin had whipped through the questions and was finished before Clementine was halfway through, so he had been excused early.

Edwin stood by the door and signaled to Clementine. She looked up, but Miss Lamb's head was bent over the test paper. He motioned again, for both haste and quiet.

Afterward Clementine wondered why she had been so quick to obey Edwin's signal without Miss Lamb's permission. But that was afterward. At the moment she did not think at all; she simply stood up and tiptoed out of the room.

"I'm a magician," he whispered. "I can wave my hand and say a secret magic formula — and disappear into thin air! Completely invisible!"

"Oh, for glory goodness!" she said, disgusted. "I thought you had something important to tell me!"

"Important? Important? I have made the most remarkable discovery in modern history, and you don't think that's important? Come here."

He motioned her to follow him down the hall and stood with his back to the closed laundry-chute door.

"Now I will begin my incantation," he said dramatically. "Shut your eyes tight, listen closely to these magic words, but whatever you do, don't peek or you'll have a spell put on you and you will fall asleep for one hundred years."

Clementine knew it was only some of Edwin's nonsense, but even so, the mysterious way he said it sent a chill up her back. One hundred years!

He began to chant softly, "Ooga, boonga, hemmelman, bay, close your eyes, I'm fading away. Do not speak and do not peek, oonga, boonga, bimmel, squeek!"

She heard the sound of a door opening — a door? — and opened her eyes just in time to see Edwin climbing over the edge of the chute.

"No! Don't do it! Edwin — " she screamed as he dropped from her view.

He screamed too, a bloodcurdling yell that echoed up from the long dark chute as he fell.

Miss Lamb heard it. Dropping her papers, she ran into the hall to find Clementine pointing at the empty hole that a moment ago had been filled with Edwin Peabody.

Nanny Ferguson and Nanny McGregor heard it. They put the babies safely in their cribs and ran down the hall. Sheila heard it on the second floor. The eerie scream came from nowhere and echoed into the master bedroom. She dropped her duster and ran, adding her shouts to all the others'.

Simpson was sorting silver in the dining room when he heard the shriek in the wall, and Kathleen in the morning room leaped in terror.

Of them all, Miss Lamb understood first what had happened. She leaned into the chute and bellowed, "Edwin!" Sheila and Mary Catherine flung open the laundry-chute door on the second floor and yelled down, "Mother of God! It's killed he is! Master Edwin, are ye alive? Oh, heaven save us!"

Simpson reached the door in the butler's pantry only seconds later and he shouted, "Who's there! What's going on?"

This was a lot of shouting, combined with strangled sobs and yelps out of the darkness, and it echoed and re-echoed up and down the long tin shaft. Clementine was already running down the stairs with Miss Lamb at her heels, and the others followed. The excited group trooped into the kitchen. Clementine jerked open the door and found — nothing! Nothing but the pile of sheets that filled the doorway. Far above her head somewhere Edwin was calling for help.

Miss Lamb clawed at the sheets and dragged out the laundry as fast as she could. The others were helping or getting in the way, and in the background Cook was screeching, "They've lost their minds, the bloomin' lot of them! What's going on? Tell me, what's going on?"

It probably seemed forever to Edwin, but in a very short time his striped legs came into view, kicking and thrashing.

"Be still!" commanded Miss Lamb. "Be still and we'll help you out." She grabbed his ankles and pulled, and he came popping out like a cork out of a

71

bottle, but much louder. She untangled him from the lace-edged sheet and set him firmly on his feet, unhurt.

"Now," she said sternly, "tell me how you could have had an accident like that! I would like an explanation!"

The uproar broke out all over again. "Oh, don't scold the dear angel, Miss Lamb," begged Sheila. "It's that scared we all were, and that glad we are he's safe."

"Indeed," said Mary Catherine, wiping her eyes, "I thought we'd never see him alive, never again!"

"You are unhurt, Master Edwin?" Simpson asked anxiously. "Move your arms and legs, my boy, and see if anything's broken."

Mrs. Culligan had grabbed up two of her precious teacakes and was urging them on him and saying over and over, "Heaven be praised! Heaven be praised!"

Edwin had emerged from the laundry chute thoroughly frightened and determined never to do such a foolish thing again. But as he got his tears under control, he realized that to most of his audience, at least, he was a hero. He took Mrs. Culligan's teacakes and smiled at his rescuers. Simpson straightened his jacket and patted his back.

"You are a brave little soldier. A terrible accident, that." Edwin nodded, his mouth too full to talk. "You must rest now, my boy. No more lessons for the rest of the day. Isn't that right, Miss Lamb? Just rest and play and get over this awful experience."

Edwin smiled again. Things had turned out better

than he had planned. "I'll just rest for a while, Miss Lamb," he said in a weak, quavering, but very noble voice. "Then I'll be back hard at work at my lessons again."

Miss Lamb gave him a long, long look. Then she said sweetly, "I understand, Edwin. You must go to your room at once. Nothing heavy for lunch — tea and dry toast is best after a bad fall. Get right into bed and, of course, no more lessons today."

He gave his enthralled audience one more brave smile and went upstairs. Clementine followed Miss Lamb to the schoolroom. She was in no mood to study. She said bitterly, "That's the way it always goes. Edwin makes trouble and somehow he always comes out ahead. It isn't fair! He gets out of lessons, and what do I get? More spelling words and sums to do."

"Don't complain, Clementine. Just pull up your stockings and get your rain cape. While our brave little soldier is resting in bed today, you and I will go out and find some adventure, rain or no rain. You can tell him all about it when we return."

Clementine could hardly believe it. "You mean — "

"I mean that Edwin will have all this long, dark, dull, boring afternoon to think things over," answered Miss Lamb serenely. "Didn't I tell you I understood something about boys?"

Chapter Seven

Fortunately Mrs. Tipton and her sister had been out shopping. They were gone all day, and when they arrived home for tea, Edwin was out of bed. No one felt it was necessary to upset his mother with the story of his mishap. The two ladies were caught up in new plans.

"This visiting and entertaining all day long must stop," Aunt Maude declared. "We will go out only in the evenings, and we must put our minds to serious matters or I shall go home again to Pittsburgh with not a stitch new to wear."

They had purchased yards and yards of beautiful fabrics of every kind, and Miss Pierce, the dressmaker, was due to arrive in the morning. The sewing room next to Edwin's bedroom on the third floor had been made ready. Miss Pierce had a sewing machine, and it was hauled up the stairs and installed in the workroom. Extra leaves had been put in the big cutting table to make it as large as possible, and there was even a platform on which the ladies could stand while their hems were being adjusted.

Clementine hoped that in the frenzy of dressmaking she would be forgotten. It was not that she didn't enjoy new clothes. Not at all; but she wished they could appear by magic, all finished, or bought, like shoes, in a store. She dreaded the whole tiresome business of having them made — the endless measurings and fittings, standing motionless or turning slowly while Mama and Aunt Maude and Miss Pierce discussed the skirt length or the fit of the collar.

And all the while Edwin would be popping his head in to announce that he was having a great time, and when would she be through?

They went through this several times a year. This year it would be worse than ever because of the centennial. But for a while, at least, Clementine didn't have to worry. Aunt Maude was to be taken care of first, and then Mama. And that would take some time.

Miss Lamb was determined that nothing would interrupt her schoolroom routine. Clementine's schoolwork was greatly improved and Miss Lamb urged her on. The sums she set for Edwin, too, were harder each day, and although he complained bitterly, he struggled along. He was bound that Clementine would not catch up to him, and he never let a chance go by to prove how much more he knew. They squabbled constantly but amiably. There were no real hard feelings between them — only rivalry.

As the weather grew nicer it was harder and harder for Clementine to keep her mind on spelling and

French and embroidery. The schoolroom was flooded with spring sunshine, and the sprays of forsythia and pussy willow that Miss Lamb had cut and put in water were a reminder that much was happening outdoors.

An impudent sparrow perched on the windowsill and chirped at the children. The warm breeze ruffled the papers on the desk. Everything seemed to be saying, "Come on, come outside, leave it all, come out!"

Clementine's winter drawers and flannel petticoat were far too hot and itchy, but Miss Lamb was firm. She had consulted with Nanny, and Nanny said, "First of May and not one day sooner! We're not about to have the little dear come down with the pneumonia." So in spite of all Clementine's complaints, the winter woolies had to be put on each day.

Their afternoon walks were more precious than ever. Clementine looked enviously at the groups of girls who played jacks on the curbstones with a fine disregard for passing wagons and carriages. The little girls who lived on Clementine's part of Spruce Street led far more sedate lives. Now that the weather was pleasant they walked to Rittenhouse Square and rolled their hoops on the broad sidewalks there, while their nannies and governesses watched and warned as soon as the fun became a little boisterous. It was not ladylike to run too fast or jump too high or — heavens above! — yell. And inside, Clementine was boiling to run and jump and yell as loudly as she could just because it was spring and she was ten years old.

Miss Lamb was not at all like the other governesses in the park, and the brisk walks that she favored were almost runs when the breezes pushed them from behind. Nor did she confine her charges to the few quiet blocks between the Tiptons' house and Rittenhouse Square. They ranged far and wide in the bustling city, sometimes so far that they had to take the horse-drawn omnibus home in order to be in time for tea. Clementine and Edwin loved that — sitting on the long benches facing the aisle, scuffing their feet in the straw that covered the floor, giggling, whispering, even shoving each other until a word from Miss Lamb put a stop to their roughhousing.

Without being told, they knew that the omnibus trips were not to be mentioned at home. Mama, Clementine was sure, had never ridden in a public omnibus in her life. Once in a long time she took a hansom cab home from an outing. But usually Pat and the Tipton carriage were waiting to take her wherever she wanted to go. She and Aunt Maude would have been shocked if they had known that their children were riding in a public conveyance, side by side with workingmen and heavily laden shoppers and who knows what else! Even Nanny would have been outraged. So they said nothing and no one was the wiser. Miss Lamb seemed to see nothing wrong in it, and even said once that a variety of experiences did one good, kept one from becoming narrow-minded.

The daily expeditions helped. But with the whole world bursting into spring around her, with the birds chirping their heads off in the trees, with the city children flocking like sparrows to the sidewalks to play, Clementine struggled to burst out of her cocoon, too. The hurdy-gurdy man on the corner cranked out his tunes, and the most Clementine could do was to drop a penny into the monkey's outstretched cap. It was not enough. She wanted to dance to his tunes, and when he moved on she wanted to go, too, to follow the urging music all over the city, to dance until she dropped.

The spring winds were bringing more than maple pollen, more than the smell of the docks and the ships from far away, more than the clamor of the city. Spring was saying to Clementine, "Break out! Run free!"

Life in the Spruce Street house had never seemed so mild, so flavorless. Clementine had little time to spend downstairs in the kitchen where blood seemed to run richer, where quarrels simmered and stewed along with the cooking. She missed Cook's bursts of oratory and profanity. Mama's guests appeared by comparison to be pale and lifeless. It was more of an effort than ever to remember her curtsies, to murmur polite replies, when, all dressed up, she was taken downstairs by Miss Lamb to greet the guests at tea.

Rebellion was brewing, but no one recognized it.

Nanny said she appeared "a mite wankley" and recommended a spring tonic. Clementine choked down the awful stuff, and her inward boiling grew only worse. Sooner or later the volcano was bound to erupt.

Spring was working its unsettling spell on Miss Lamb, too, although she kept her feelings well-hidden. On one of their walks a young lady carrying a sign that read *Women Unite for Freedom!* had stopped the governess and handed her an advertising card.

"Do try to attend," she urged. "You will find the lecturer most enlightening. And it's convenient — right on the square."

Most of the ladies she approached had looked amused or indignant, and some had torn up the card angrily and scattered the pieces in the street. But Miss Lamb read it thoughtfully and tucked it in her purse. From time to time she took out the little paper and looked at it again, and each time she wore a more determined expression.

"I'll do it," she finally said aloud. "I'll go. Tomorrow will be my afternoon out, children."

It had been arranged that Miss Lamb was to have every third Thursday off, but so far she had not taken advantage of the privilege. Clementine and Edwin were startled.

"Our walk — " they said in unison.

"You can walk with the nannies and the babies," she answered firmly. "I am going to attend a lecture."

She announced her intentions to Nanny McGregor,

and Nanny agreed that it was high time she had a change. "Run along to your lecture, my dear, if that kind of thing is to your taste. Nanny Ferguson and I will keep a sharp eye on those two, never you fear. They can help us entertain the little ones."

Entertaining the little ones had been good enough for stormy winter weather, but for this particular day, with the sun shining and a strong breeze blowing, it was too tame to be considered.

"Miss Lamb insists we get fresh air every day for our health," said Edwin piously.

"And so you shall, my sweeties, as soon as the babies wake from their naps. You may help us push the carriages."

"Well, while they're still sleeping, may we go out? Just between here and the square?"

Nanny McGregor considered this.

"Oh, I guess no great harm could come of a trip to the square," she agreed comfortably. "Remember, don't speak to strangers or pet any mad dogs, and look both ways as you cross the street. But no farther away than the square, remember."

It certainly didn't sound very exciting to Clementine, but it was better than waiting for the babies to get up, squalling and wet, from their naps. Edwin, however, looked as if Nanny had given him the nicest of presents. He gave her ample waist a hug so fierce it left her gasping, grabbed Clementine's hand, and dragged her down the stairs.

"Hurry!" he panted. "I've got an idea!"

Usually Edwin's ideas gave his cousin a cold chill of anxiety, but today she was ready for anything.

"Come on. We're going to rent a horse!"

She stopped on the sidewalk in absolute amazement.

"Come on," he said again. "Don't just stand there wasting the afternoon. We're going to rent a horse and carriage!"

"Edwin, you are out of your mind. We've only twenty-three cents between us, and twenty of that is mine."

"We don't need money, stupid. We go to the livery stable and say, 'Put it on Mr. Horace Tipton's bill.' I know; I watched how Pat did it."

Her mouth still hung open in surprise.

"Come on, you ninny! I've figured it all out. Nanny said we couldn't go any farther than the square, didn't she? So we won't. The livery stable is in between, so there! Ah, don't be a spoilsport, Clem. Think what fun we'll have driving round and round the square."

It was just what Clementine wanted and she needed no further urging. Her conscience pricked her a little as she trotted along at Edwin's side, but she ignored it and said eagerly, "You're right, Edwin. We won't go farther than the square, and we won't pet any mad dogs, or speak to strangers, so no one can say we've disobeyed. And nobody will even guess what we've been up to."

At the stable she let Edwin take the lead.

"We'll have a horse and carriage, please," he said grandly. "It's to go on my uncle Horace Tipton's bill."

"Well — " said the stable boy doubtfully.

"A fast horse," Edwin said. Clementine shivered with excitement.

"Don't have none in right now," said the stable boy. "Only old Bess, here, slow as molasses. Unless your uncle'd want to wait — but there's Pinchy. He's a pony, but lively as you could ask for. Would your uncle take him?"

"I believe he would." Edwin was still very grand and high-toned. "As long as the beast is lively and moves right along. We've no time to waste."

"Then he'll want the pony cart, too." The obliging young man wheeled out a light wicker cart and hitched up Pinchy. "A nice fast rig," he said.

"Very good," said Edwin, smooth as silk. "It will do just fine, I'm sure. My uncle enjoys a snappy drive."

That was true. So far Edwin had not told one lie — just pulled the truth around to fit his needs. Clementine knew what Miss Lamb would say to this kind of evasion. Then she put Miss Lamb right out of her head. This was going to be an afternoon to enjoy.

Edwin insisted that he drive. "Uncle Horace would feel safer if I brought it round," he said to her for the benefit of the stable boy, and Clementine allowed him to take the reins. It was only fair that he should have

the first turn, since he had thought of the wonderful plan.

They clattered out of the stable. "We'll bow and smile and you must tip your cap to people," she said to Edwin. "We'll do this in style."

The pony was feeling springlike, too. He pranced

and shied, and the light basket cart swung from side to side.

"Are you sure you know how?" she asked as they lurched around the corner. Edwin was too busy tugging on the reins to answer. In a moment his persistent pulling won out, and Pinchy settled down to a fast trot. The light pony cart bounced along and Clementine held on tightly with one hand to keep her balance. Edwin urged the pony on, and they whisked in and out of the slow afternoon traffic. They went so fast Clementine's hat ribbons blew straight out behind, and she was thankful her new spring hat was well fastened on.

She waved her free hand regally and bowed to everyone. They passed several people she knew and she hoped they were going fast enough so that she and Edwin had not been recognized. And then she didn't care. The spring afternoon went to her head as completely as it had to Edwin's.

After many fast turns around Rittenhouse Square she began to tire of bowing and waving. "Now it's my turn to drive," she said.

At that moment a heavy carriage swung in ahead of them and the high wheel grazed the cart. Edwin hung on, and with a lot of yelling finally turned Pinchy out of the near collision.

"You can't! It's a job for a man!" he panted. "Pinchy won't mind a girl. Anyway, I thought of it!"

It was an outrage. It was more than Clementine could bear. With a bellow that surprised even herself, she gave Edwin a sharp jab in the ribs with her elbow. He winced and turned to look at her, and in that instant she grabbed the reins out of his startled hands.

Clementine Tipton had taken charge.

Chapter Eight

*I*t *was wonderful!* The feeling of flying along, of mastery over the lively pony, of the swift clatter of hooves and rumble of wheels along the paving stones, the sway of the light cart — it was infinitely more exciting than just being a passenger. Just holding the reins in her hands made all the difference.

She maneuvered a fast turn onto Walnut Street on the north side of the square. "See," she yelled at Edwin, "I can drive as well as you can!" She slapped the reins with a flourish and urged Pinchy to go faster. He responded by breaking out of his fast trot into a wild gallop.

The sedate afternoon traffic around Rittenhouse Square could not accommodate such speed. The cart lurched and bounced, and Clementine and Edwin both shouted, "Whoa! Slow down!"

But Pinchy plunged on.

"He's running away," panted Clementine, pulling with all her might on the reins. Pinchy only increased his speed as they rounded the next corner, and Clementine lost her balance. As she fell backward Edwin grabbed for the reins. He managed to get a firm grip on one of them. He jerked wildly, and Pinchy swerved suddenly, up over the curb.

Edwin saw the hitching post, but he was no longer steering, just struggling to hang on. The cart wheel caught on the post, the wheel ripped off, the whole basket lurched over, and Clementine and Edwin slid out in a pile of wicker wreckage.

The ruined mess of basketry bumped along behind Pinchy for a few yards more before Clementine could recover and struggle to her feet. Edwin was hopelessly tangled, with one foot through the broken side of the cart and one rein caught around his arm.

"Stop, you idiot!" she bellowed at the confused pony. "Stop, you limb of the devil, you spawn of a misbegotten bastard! Whoa! Whoa!"

Every choice expression she had ever heard from Mrs. Culligan came roaring out now. The little horse seemed to recognize the sound of authority in her bellow, and he bumped obediently to a stop.

Their wild trip around the square had of course attracted attention, and at the sound of the crash a crowd began to gather. Children ran to see, and nannies ran to keep them out of trouble. The little pet dogs ran after them, the policeman who usually flirted with the nannies and patted good children on the head suddenly had something official to do.

Clementine and Edwin had been much too busy to notice, but as they made their final sweep around the square, a group of ladies was leaving one of the brownstone houses on the Walnut Street side. They were talking earnestly as they came down the steps, and for a moment they were too absorbed to observe the confusion. Clementine's shouts blasted their ears, and they turned in amazement to look. Then, in midsentence, one of the ladies left the group and ran toward the wreck.

It was Miss Lamb.

Without a word she clapped a hand over Clementine's mouth; with the other hand she hauled Edwin to his feet. She checked quickly to see that neither child was hurt, and grimly removed the remains of the wicker-basket cart from around Edwin's leg.

Pinchy's wild race was over. He stood at the curb, staring back curiously at what was left of the cart, and looking as if he had never gone faster than a walk in all his life.

"Stimson's livery?" Miss Lamb asked. They both nodded. Without another word Miss Lamb picked up the reins, motioned for the children to follow, clucked to the pony, and started off to the livery stable. The broken, one-wheeled wreck dragged behind. They left the square, all three looking straight ahead with never a sign that they noticed the hoots and excitement that followed them.

Only a short while before Clementine had felt free, exhilarated, light as a bubble, somehow quicker and more clever than ordinary mortals. And now it was all over. She plodded along behind Miss Lamb, sluggish and dull. Yet the sun was still shining, the breeze still tugged at her hat, ruffled her hair. Nothing had changed, but everything had changed. Spring had deserted her.

Without speaking to the children Miss Lamb returned the pony and the broken pieces of cart. She explained that Mr. Tipton would settle for the damages. Then they walked home in silence. Still in absolute silence she indicated that they were to wash and change.

Tea came, but neither Clementine nor Edwin could choke down a bite and even Miss Lamb seemed to be having difficulty.

"I would like an explanation," she said finally.

Edwin and Clementine told their story, plain and bald, no elaborations. Edwin took the blame for thinking of the idea and Clementine quickly added that she had made no objections. It was hard to look back and remember what a beautiful inspiration Edwin's idea had seemed.

"Had you money enough to hire a pony and cart?"

Miserably they shook their heads. "I said to put it on Uncle Horace's bill," whispered Edwin.

"Without his permission?"

They nodded.

"We must discuss this with Mr. Tipton," she said sternly. Obediently they rose and followed her down the stairs to the library. Clementine was too sore and shaken and ashamed to be frightened. It didn't seem to matter what Papa said. No punishment would be severe enough to suit the enormity of their crime.

They met Simpson in the hall and Miss Lamb asked that he announce them.

"All of you?"

"All of us."

"Nothing serious, I hope?" he asked anxiously. "If it is only a small matter — a childish mistake, so to speak — maybe I could handle it. No need to trouble the master, don't you know?"

"Thank you, Simpson, but this was no childish mistake. It was a terrible mistake. No, I will have to speak to Mr. Tipton."

Simpson sighed and did as he was asked. In a moment he was back in the hall again. "You're to go in, Miss Lamb, and whatever it is, be careful. The old man's with him, and that always makes him contentious."

Grandpa Tipton! Clementine did not even know that her grandfather had dropped in for one of his infrequent visits. Simpson was right. Grandpa had a way of provoking Papa that always made him cross.

Mr. Tipton and his father turned as the three entered the room. Papa was stout and tall and Grandpa was stout and short, but except for the difference in height they looked rather alike. They didn't think at all alike, though, and hardly ever agreed on anything. They had been arguing about something; that was evi-

dent. Both men were rather red in the face and wore fierce expressions. They both seemed to welcome the interruption.

"Well, now, Miss Lamb, this is a pleasure. I believe you have not met my father, Mr. Titus Tipton. This is Miss Lamb, Father, Clementine's very capable new governess. Do sit down, all of you."

Grandpa leaned forward and peered at Miss Lamb, and then said exactly what came into his mind, just as he always did.

"Pretty little thing, aren't you? English, I hear — but you're not much more than a child yourself! Can you manage my wildcat granddaughter?"

Clementine's heart sank. They weren't off to a very good beginning.

Papa answered quickly, "There you go again, Father! It's just as I said; you always know the last word! Miss Lamb has proved herself to be a remarkable teacher, and I understand Clementine has made fine progress."

"Anybody'd be better than that Frenchwoman. A stiff broom, she was; only thing she knew was curtsying and smirking. You, Miss Lamb, are you going to make my Clem into an imitation of a girl, or will you let her be a real person, eh?"

Papa said, "Father, please restrain yourself. Miss Lamb is an excellent teacher, excellent." He chomped angrily on his cigar.

Grandpa leaned back in his chair and said, "Glad to

hear it; indeed I am. Maybe your judgment is improving at last, boy. So the children are behaving, eh, Miss Lamb?"

"Well, sir," she answered, her voice trembling only a little, "that is what we have come to discuss. A dreadful thing has happened, and we are all three equally to blame."

Clementine and Edwin looked at each other. How was Miss Lamb to blame?

"I was away for part of the afternoon, sir, and while I was gone Edwin and Clementine took it upon themselves to rent a pony and cart from Stimson's Livery Stable and drive it around the square."

Papa smiled. "Come now, Miss Lamb, that isn't too bad. Worse things than that have happened."

"Worse things did happen, sir. They had no money to spend, so they hired it in your name. They had an accident — the pony was unharmed and fortunately so were the children — but the cart is wrecked beyond repair. The bill will be considerable."

Papa stopped smiling. "Without-my-permission they hired and wrecked — and what were you doing all this time, Miss Lamb?"

Miss Lamb looked him straight in the eye and said, "As I said, sir, I consider myself quite as much to blame as the children. I was taking my afternoon off, sir, to which I am entitled as you know, every third Thursday. And for that I make no apology. My error was in leaving the children without definite plans to occupy their time until I returned. It is for this reason that I propose to have you withhold my wages each month until the cart is paid for."

"Can't be more fair than that, Horace. You won't lose a cent."

Papa said, "Father, it is not the money I am concerned with; it's the principle of the thing."

"Ha! Any time anybody says it's not the money but the principle, you can be sure it's the money. You've always been something of a skinflint, boy. Now admit it."

Clementine wished fervently that Grandpa wouldn't tease Papa so. It would only make a bad situation worse. She spoke up, hoping to help Miss Lamb's case.

"Papa, Miss Lamb didn't know anything about this. It's just not fair if she has to pay for the cart. Keep my spending money and" — she poked Edwin in the ribs so he nodded in agreement — "Edwin's, too, and we'll pay for the cart if it takes years."

Grandpa chuckled. "That's a generous offer, Horace. You'll have a bit coming in for your old age."

Papa appeared to control his impatience with a real effort. "Father, for the last time, I tell you it is not the money for the damaged cart I am concerned with. How do I know a thing like this won't happen again? Miss Lamb was careless enough to neglect her duty and go off to — Where did you say you went, Miss Lamb?"

"To a lecture, Mr. Tipton."

"A lecture? A lecture about what?"

"About women's rights, sir. It was very interesting."

If Miss Lamb had dropped a stick of lighted dynamite in the quiet library, she would not have produced more of an explosion.

"Women's rights! A member of my household at a lecture on women's rights! That — that rag-taggled bunch of trouble-making idiots, those — those — "

Words failed him. He jumped to his feet and stamped back and forth, unable to contain himself. Grandpa Tipton threw back his head and laughed. His round belly jiggled under his tightly buttoned waistcoat. He laughed until he had to stop and blow his nose.

Miss Lamb sat very straight and tightened her lips. She did not think that anything was funny. Neither did Papa.

"Miss Lamb, I must demand that you never again attend such a meeting while you are in my employ. You are new here; perhaps you did not really understand the enormity of your unbecoming behavior. Just see that it never happens again."

"There was nothing at all unbecoming about the meeting, Mr. Tipton. It was conducted in a very ladylike manner."

Papa got red in the face again, and then regained his control. "Miss Lamb," he began in a calm, reasonable tone of voice, "if you stop to think about this rubbish, if you will use your intelligence — which I sincerely believe is fairly high for a woman — you will not be taken in by the arguments of a few foolish old biddies — "

Now it was Miss Lamb's turn to be angry. She stood up, drew herself to her full height, and said hotly, "My intelligence is fairly high for a *person,* and I am quite capable of thinking for myself. As for your opinion of the women's rights movement, it is based on ignorance. I suggest you do a little studying. And if I am to remain here as Clementine's governess, I think you should know that I believe completely in women's rights! Come, children."

She swept them out of the room, and closed the library door with what was very close to a slam. Just outside, Simpson straightened up hastily.

"For shame, Mr. Simpson! Listening at keyholes!"

"Oh, Miss Lamb," he whispered sympathetically, "I shall be so sorry to see you go."

Chapter Nine

*C*lementine *tossed and turned* and punched her pillow and turned again, but sleep would not come. She was tired enough, but there was too much to think about. She said to herself, "For want of a nail, a shoe was lost; for want of a shoe, a horse was lost." And for want of some good common sense from Clementine Tipton, Miss Lamb would be lost, too. She felt terrible. And yet it was hard to forget those few wonderful moments when everything was going so well, when Pinchy was sweeping around the corner obeying her touch on the reins.

There was still a crack of light under Miss Lamb's door. She often read late, but tonight she wasn't reading. Clementine could hear the floorboards creak as her governess paced back and forth.

Clementine's door groaned on its hinges, and she heard Edwin's voice.

"Clem," he whispered, "I can't sleep for worrying."

"Neither can I," she wailed. "Oh, Edwin!"

She hadn't cried at all when she fell out of the cart, but now she couldn't stop.

Miss Lamb was there in an instant, stumbling over Edwin in the dark.

"I'm so sorry," Clementine hiccupped. "We just never dreamed it would turn out this way —"

Edwin said, "It was all my fault. I thought of it and talked Clem into it — and now — " his voice broke, and even in the darkness Clementine knew he was crying, too. There was the quick flare of a match, and then the lamp by Clementine's bed blossomed into brightness.

"Well, for goodness sake! We can't have this! Clementine, Edwin, stop this nonsense, both of you."

They tried, but it was no use. Once they had begun, neither one could stop.

"All right, then, we'll have to talk about it, but it's too cold in here. Edwin, are you barefooted? Slippers, at once, do you hear? And a quilt. I'll poke up the fire a bit in the schoolroom and make some tea."

Wrapped in quilts, the two children trailed after Miss Lamb. She set down the lamp and poked vigorously at the fire in the stove. It had been banked for the night with fresh coal heaped up over the heart of the burning embers. A rattle of the shaker, a good stirring with the poker, and soon the flames were leaping again.

Clementine and Edwin were quiet by now with only an occasional hiccup that escaped in spite of themselves.

"Now," said Miss Lamb, "let's get a few things straightened out —"

Before she could finish, they heard the stairs creaking, the hall door opened and a hoarse whisper, "Give me a hand, somebody, afore I drop this whole shebang!"

"Mr. Tipton!" Miss Lamb sprang up and ran to Grandpa Tipton's aid.

"Sshh," he warned. "The hornet's nest below is still buzzing, and the chief hornet is after me, too. How in thunderation do the maids manage these trays, I wonder?" He set the big tray down with a thump. "There, I made it, and not too much spilled. Hot milk and muffins, children, and tea for me and Lambie, here. Cook sent up jam, too, the old heathen, and apples all around."

Clementine's eyes grew wide. No one, no one had ever called her governess anything but Miss Lamb, and here was Grandpa calling her Lambie, just like that. It certainly had turned out to be a day of surprises. Miss Lamb didn't seem to mind, or if she did she didn't show it. She just smiled and said, "What a nice thought. Just what we needed most," and poured the milk into the cups.

"Simpson told me the three of you didn't eat enough supper to keep a sparrow alive. I thought you could do with a spot of comfort, and maybe some cheering up. Things aren't as bad as you think, so let me see some smiles."

All three stared at him, solemn as owls.

"Well, now, I'll explain, and then maybe you'll smile for me. Miss Lamb is to stay, if she's a mind to, after the way my son carried on. And Clementine and Edwin, you are to pay the livery-stable bill with your pocket money each week. At that rate, I figure you'll be paying it off when you're as old as I am, but you might just learn to think twice before you do such a thing again. Now, how's that?"

"Oh, Mr. Tipton, I do thank you!"

"Don't thank me, Lambie, my child. It was Mrs. Tipton who had conniptions at the thought of finding a new governess. She persuaded Horace that you should stay on in spite of your dangerous ideas."

"Dangerous ideas?" Miss Lamb asked indignantly.

"Sounded dangerous to her. And Horace, of course, was fit to be tied. You couldn't have picked a worse day to bring up the mention of women's rights. Not after the news Horace got today."

"News?"

"Seems the women's committee, acting on the premise that women are capable of making decisions, had sometime ago written to the composer Wagner and asked him to compose a special piece of music just for the opening of the centennial. The word was brought to Horace today that Wagner agreed to it, and the music will be ready for opening day. You can't think how upset Horace is!"

"But Mr. Wagner's music is highly thought of — "

"Oh, he's not angry about the music. Horace likes a good tune — But the idea of it. He's burned to a crisp that he didn't think of it himself. To think that the women's committee thought up the plan and carried it through, raised every penny of the cost themselves — and it cost a pretty penny, too — and never even asked the men's advice, much less their permission. Horace says the next thing will be the country — that women will think they can vote and run the country, and he's convinced they'll run it right down the drain." He stopped for a drink of tea. "Can't say I agree with him. A few good smart women couldn't make a worse mess than we've got in politics today, and they just might do better."

"They might, indeed."

Clementine was amazed. Women in politics? She had heard her father talk about politics, and it didn't sound like something a woman should do.

"At any rate, it's a sensitive point with Horace, you can see. I suppose I shouldn't be surprised. Bring up a child to be a proper little society prig, and that's what you'll get. I wish I had started younger to shake him loose from some of his ideas — make him laugh at himself a little."

He looked sadly into his teacup as if he might find the secret of child-rearing there. Then he said, "Well, now, what they want from you is your promise that you'll not publicly espouse the cause of women, and so be an embarrassment to the board of directors of the centennial. You can believe what you want on your own time. Agreed?"

She nodded. It seemed fair enough.

"Now let's talk of other things. Tell me how you happened to come here, so far away from your home."

Clementine had completely forgotten that moment on the day of Miss Lamb's arrival, but now it all came back to her. She burst out in a rush, "Oh, tell it! You promised — about how a black bull brought you here! You said some day when there wasn't much to laugh about — "

"Hush, child, you'll wake the babies, and the nannies will be in to scold us all."

Clementine lowered her voice. "Please?" she begged. "We need to laugh a little."

Edwin and Clementine hitched their chairs closer and tucked their quilts around them. Miss Lamb was very fussy about bedtimes, and allowed no lingering once the clock had struck. And here they were, sitting up by the schoolroom stove with the clock ticking away absolutely unnoticed. It had been a mixed-up day all around. They waited breathlessly for Miss Lamb to begin.

"I'm trying to think how it all came about," she said. "I'll have to go back a bit to get it all straight."

"Start with the bull," prompted Edwin. Clementine jabbed him in the ribs with her elbow. "Sshh!" The jab did not hurt him through the folds of his quilt, but he shushed and waited.

"Well," she began in a dreamy remembering voice, "my home is in the village of Wickham, and you must understand that it is a very small village, hardly more than a cluster of buildings around the green. An inn, a few houses, the church, and that is all. Farms and woods and fields all round, rather poor country, but lovely. My father is the vicar of the church there, and we lived in the parish house across the green — ten of us, eight children, crowded in a house that would have served five better. Father always says he is poor in worldly goods but rich in family. It is a fine sentiment, but even if my father were rich he would empty his pockets to help some poor farmer whose crop had failed, and then he'd be poor again. So, to augment his scanty income, Father teaches school as well. Only a few paying students — Lady Alice sent her sons, one or two others from the village, my three brothers, and the five of us girls when our mama could spare us from the housework.

"It was discovered that I had a natural bent for books and I learned fast. When I was hardly older than these children here I had gone as far and as fast as the big boys, and I was trusted to teach the very little ones their ABCs and easy sums. So the years went by, one much like the other, with always a new crop of young ones coming along, for Lord Cullen and Lady Alice had a very large family. Their boys were so naughty that tutors could not be persuaded to stay, especially in a rather run-down manor house, so deep in the country. So they were sent to Father to learn.

"I began to wonder what would become of me. I grew moody and restless and discontented. As the boys grew older they went on to higher schools or out into the world. My brothers all went to divinity schools where they were given scholarships. But for the girls nothing was planned but to follow our mother's ways into housewifery, cleaning and cooking and cheese-making and tending the garden."

"Not a bad life," commented Grandpa quietly.

"Not a bad life at all," Miss Lamb answered, "but I had this terrible yearning to use my mind, to spread my wings and fly. I wasn't ready at eighteen to settle down and be a good wife. And what's more, when I looked around for husband material, I felt trapped. A few young farmers, an elderly widower, and the inn-keeper's stupid son. Not for me. I was trying to resign myself — and not very successfully — to the quiet life of a spinster daughter, when Fate came to my rescue in the shape of the black bull Orion.

"At this time the youngest child coming to my father was Timothy, only five. Timothy was, and is, a bright, lively, spoiled, disruptive boy, and my father turned him over to my care almost exclusively. With patience and firmness I was able to tame him a trifle. Lady Alice, who is a fine person but definitely lacking in both firmness and patience, was delighted. Little Timothy was the apple of her adoring eye and she was pleased that he was making progress in his lessons —

at what cost to me you will never believe," Miss Lamb added, holding her head as if it ached to remember.

"For his part, Lord Cullen saw no real need for more than the most elementary lessons, for he spent most of his life on horseback and assumed that everyone else felt as he did. But he was willing that Timothy be educated, if that was his wife's will.

"One day after Timothy was dismissed from his lessons I observed that his eyes sparkled in a particular way that meant he had thought of a new and forbidden prank. I noticed that as he left the parish house he turned to the left instead of to the right. He was taking the long way home, evidently, and had some mischief up his sleeve.

"I took my bonnet and shawl and went out, keeping him just in sight. He never looked back — he was too intent on his plan. He cut across the pastures directly to the small field that held Orion, Lord Cullen's fierce black bull. The fence was high, but Timothy climbed it as easily as if it were a ladder. At the top he paused to take off his little red jacket, tucked it under his arm, and jumped down into Orion's pen.

"Now this bull was a magnificent animal, but his temper was notorious. Touchy in the extreme. The stablemen who handled him did so with caution, and here was Timothy prancing toward the creature waving his red jacket.

"I ran across the open field, my heart in my mouth, yelling, 'Timothy! Come back!' At first Orion was

106

grazing peacefully. He paid no attention to Timothy's motions. I called again, trying to shout loudly enough to make the boy hear, and softly enough not to startle the bull. You must believe my heart was thumping so hard I thought Orion would surely hear it, too.

"Timothy is a bright lad, but stubborn as can be. He waved me away, shouting, 'I'm a bull fighter! Watch!' Orion raised his huge head and pawed the ground. By now I was staring horrified through the bars of the fence. No one was in sight, no stableman or groom. Timmy waved his jacket again and Orion twitched angrily. Once more, and the bull bellowed a furious warning. He tore at the turf with his sharp hooves and backed off, ready to charge.

"I assure you, I was not brave. I was never more frightened in my life, but I had no choice. I dropped my shawl, climbed over the fence in a flash — a country girl learns to do these boyish things," she said apologetically to Grandpa Tipton. "I felt a rip as I jumped down and ran. Fear made me fleet-footed. I never ran so fast. I scooped Timothy up just in time right from under Orion's nose, and ran with him to the fence. The bull was confused, and hesitated just long enough for me to leap for the fence. I heaved Timothy up and he clung to the top rail as I climbed. At the top I gave him a push, and I jumped, and both of us landed safely outside in the pasture grass.

"I checked to see if Timothy was hurt from the fall, and was suddenly aware of a breeziness around my legs. I heard shouts and saw the stable boys running. They were too late to save Timmy, but just in time to witness my humiliation. I looked down to see my skirt quite gone — it was hanging on a nail in the fence — and my — the back of my undergarments ripped. Your pardon, Mr. Tipton, I shouldn't speak of such things at all, but the story demands it. I was rooted to the ground, unable to move. I dared not turn my back to run, for the view from the back was even more revealing."

Grandpa Tipton was trying hard not to laugh, and he covered his face as if he were blowing his nose.

"The stable boys turned to check on Timothy, and in that instant I grabbed my shawl from the ground, wrapped it around me and ran as fast as I could for home.

"An hour later a servant from the manor house brought a neatly wrapped package — I later opened it to find my bonnet and my torn skirt — and a note from Lady Alice. The serving man kept a solemn face, but his lips twitched as if he wanted to laugh. Everyone knew, I was sure, and it would be a long time before they stopped snickering. I replied with as much dignity as I could muster that I would present myself at the manor house that afternoon as Her Ladyship requested. If I had had my way I would never have been seen in Wickham again, but I had to do as she bid.

"The butler winked as he opened the door, the little

maid giggled, I was red as a beet and stumbled all over my feet in my discomfiture.

"Well, to shorten a very long dull tale, Lady Alice embraced me with tears of gratitude for saving her adored son's life, complimented me on my cool bravery — I had been neither cool nor brave, really — and over my protests Lord Cullen insisted on giving me a reward. It was a very pretty little purse, and to my amazement when I opened it at home I found it stuffed with banknotes.

"Then and there I decided I would go away. I would shake the dust of Wickham from my shoes and venture out into the world a little before I settled down for life as a spinster schoolteacher. So here I am," she said, "thanks to Orion, and here are you children up hours after your bedtime. Into bed, and not a minute to waste!"

"But, but — " they said, trying to stretch the evening out a little longer.

"Not a minute, I said. Say goodnight to your grandfather and run."

She spoke severely, but she hugged each child in an unexpected burst of affection. It had been an unusual day all around.

Chapter Ten

L ife went on quietly and smoothly for the next few days. Mama and Aunt Maude spent their days in the sewing room with Miss Pierce and her niece Emma Garland. They ventured out only to pay a few absolutely necessary calls in the afternoon or to hurry to Chestnut Street for matching fans or velvet ribbons or French silk roses in just the right color.

And then another event came to change plans and send almost the entire household into a state of feverish excitement.

Papa and Grandpa Tipton were having breakfast one morning. Papa was reading his mail as he drank his coffee, just as he always did, when suddenly, as he opened one letter, he leaped up and yelped as if he had been bitten. It was so completely unlike Papa, and so unexpected that Simpson let the coffeepot drop with a clatter. Papa didn't even notice his stammered apologies. He was already running for the stairs, shouting, "Olympia! Olympia!"

As Simpson explained later in the kitchen, he almost

dropped the muffin tray, too, but recovered in time to mop up the tablecloth and put a platter over the mess.

Mama was coming down the stairs and was so startled by her husband's bellow that she flew down and landed in a heap in his outstretched arms.

"Wha-what?" she gasped. "Horace, are you ill? What is it?"

He hugged her publicly, quite contrary to his usual sedate behavior, and swung her around, shouting, "The Emperor! The Emperor! We've got the Emperor! Maude, where are you? Get down here! We've got the Emperor! Olympia, your husband has captured the Emperor!"

Aunt Maude was late for breakfast, as always, and was not really dressed, but in her excitement she raced out of her room with her hair mussed, her combing jacket still on and not a sign of a morning cap.

"Are you mad, Horace Tipton? Is he mad, Olympia? What is going on?"

Simpson had rung the bell in the nursery only minutes before, so the nannies had already started their stately descent with the little ones, all dressed for their breakfast visit with Mr. Tipton. Titus escaped from Nanny McGregor's hand and clumped down to see what was happening.

At the first sound of excitement, Clementine and Edwin had joined the rush. So it was quite a crowd that gathered in the hall to hear Horace Tipton's news.

"The Emperor of Brazil, Dom Pedro," he explained, "has agreed to share the honors of opening the Centennial Exposition with President Grant, and — and — listen to this — he has also accepted the invitation to dinner at the home of Mr. and Mrs. Horace Tipton the evening before the fair opens. Olympia, we've captured the Emperor!"

The news left some of his audience suitably impressed but hardly excited. But other — Mama and Aunt Maude and Simpson, who was hovering in the background so as not to miss a word — understood how stupendous the news really was.

Mama grew faint and had to have water. Aunt Maude clutched her forehead and moaned, "Olympia, our gowns simply will not *do!* Those pink roses on my white silk are just not enough!"

Simpson was rather pale at the thought of all the work an emperor would cause, but he smiled bravely. Nanny McGregor murmured to Nanny Ferguson, "They must both have new lace caps with blue and pink ribbons. Their best long dresses will be fine. And Titus will wear his dear little sailor outfit," as if the Emperor would surely be calling in the nursery.

After Grandpa Tipton heard what the excitement was all about, he returned to the breakfast room again and went to work on the platter of lamb chops.

"Breakfast'll get cold," he called. But even when they all came trooping into the room, no one was interested in food.

"Olympia, you look a mite peaked. Try some of this ham; Cook's outdone herself."

"I'm far too excited to eat, Father Tipton. I declare, an emperor! And coming to our house! Horace, how does one address an emperor? We'll curtsy, of course, but how deep a curtsy? We must all practice backing out of the room. One never turns one's back on royalty, I've heard. Is there an empress? Gracious, I feel faint again. Oh my!" She leaned her head on her hands.

"Of course you feel faint. All this foolish gibble-gabble and not a bite to eat. Here." Grandpa Tipton buttered a muffin lavishly and handed it to her. "Eat this and drink some tea and your head'll clear all right."

"There's so much to do to get ready," Aunt Maude was moaning again. "So much to plan — we'll just have to work night and day!"

"Well, you all can if you've a mind to. But count me out," said Grandpa bluntly. "My Sunday suit'll do fine, and my Sunday handshake, too. I'll shake the fellow's hand and say pleased to meet you, and I'll turn and walk away when I'm ready. He'll get my best American manners and no more."

Papa bristled at his father's tone.

"This is no ordinary American we'll be entertaining, Father. He is royalty and will expect to be treated as such."

"Well, I'm no ordinary American, either," Grandpa

Tipton said stubbornly, waving his fork for emphasis. "No American is ordinary, to my mind. If this Emperor fellow wants bowing and scraping he should stay at home where he'll get it. What's more, I'm ashamed that any son of mine would take on so over a bit of two-penny Your Highness or Your Excellency or whatever."

"I'm not taking on, as you call it, Father," said Papa, his voice rising.

"I don't know what you call it then," Grandpa shouted. "You're in such a flap you can't sit still, as het-up as a child with a new balloon. Come down to earth, boy, and get your good sense back, if you ever had any!"

"Sense! You think it didn't take any sense to arrange a thing like this? To snatch an emperor right out from under every other nose in Philadelphia?"

"That's just what I'm talking about. I'd think shame to go to all this effort for a title and some gold braid. You're an American, dammit, and this is our country's hundredth birthday — and you've forgotten how we fought to get away from just such — "

"Sshh, Father Tipton," Mama implored. "Not in front of the children."

"Don't try to shush me, Olympia. I'll have my say and then I'll leave. And I won't be back until your royal stuffed popinjay has left!"

At the first sound of an argument the nannies had quietly faded out of the room, dragging Titus along.

114

Nanny McGregor flashed a look at Clementine and Edwin that meant, "Come along this instant!" But they ignored it. Arguments between Papa and Grandpa were always loud and lively, and a nice change in this house where most conversations were carried out in a polite murmur. Besides, Clementine had long learned that the quarrels between them were almost a habit, and that both of them said many things they didn't really mean.

Papa yelled back, "Don't call him a royal stuffed popinjay! You're a stubborn old fool! You always have been and always will be! You can go or stay, just as you like!"

Grandpa slammed back his chair and jumped up.

"This is one fool who'll not be making a monkey out of himself backing and curtsying. I won't grovel for any living man. And as for you, Horace, it's my opinion that you are completely off your katoot!" He stamped out of the morning room and upstairs in a towering rage.

Clementine and Edwin had taken advantage of the commotion to settle down at the table and quickly load their plates. They had had porridge and cocoa in the nursery and weren't really hungry. But the platter of browned sausages looked so appetizing that they dug in while they had a chance. Simpson noticed, of course. Simpson noticed everything, and he quietly stacked pancakes on their plates. His hand trembled slightly as he poured the maple syrup — loud argu-

ments between the two Mr. Tiptons always upset him
— but no one else was even bothered.

Aunt Maude nibbled on a muffin as she paced up and
down. She planned aloud the changes that would have
to be made in their centennial outfits.

"Violet silk, a bluish violet, don't you think, Olympia dear? And a parasol of deeper violet, and gray
gloves — "

Mama didn't even hear. She had skipped breakfast
entirely and was already at her writing desk, making
lists.

"There'll be so many invitations to write. Shall we
ask the Bloomingtons? No, they're too dull and fusty
and — Yes, on the other hand, we shall have to ask
them because of the Logans. Oh, dear!"

Papa finished his last cup of coffee and asked Simpson to send Pat up right away.

"We'll go out to the fair grounds," he said. "It is
very important that everything be done on time."

"Not to business, sir?" Simpson was shocked.

"Hang the business, Simpson," said Papa grandly.
"There'll be plenty of time for business later. The
centennial must go on!"

It seemed to Clementine a good day to ask for
special privileges since everyone was so distraught.
"May we go along, Papa?" she begged. "Edwin and I?
Please."

He thought about it for a second as he was drawing
on his gloves. "No," he decided. "Another day. It is

important that I not be distracted. I must check on every detail."

He bowed to Mama and Aunt Maude and took his top hat from Simpson. "Good day, my dears. We all have much to do." And he was off, humming happily under his breath.

Sheila came in to announce that Miss Pierce and her niece had arrived and were already beginning work in the sewing room, and would Mrs. Tipton and Mrs. Peabody be available for fittings soon. Aunt Maude left her muffin and Mama her lists and they hurried upstairs, talking excitedly.

Simpson drew a deep breath and shook his head. He looked at the last survivors of the stormy breakfast.

"Run along if you've finished," he said. "There'll be a meeting with Cook before long to plan the menu, and I must get this room in order. Stay out from underfoot today, and no tricks, mind you. There's confusion enough around here."

Clementine and Edwin had eaten all they could hold and more. They puffed slowly up the two long flights of steps to the schoolroom.

They started to tell Miss Lamb about the morning's excitement, but she cut them off crisply. "That's gossip, children. Family information. We won't discuss it. Open your copybooks and we'll begin on the lesson for the day."

It didn't seem fair that they should be expected to carry on as usual when so much was going on below.

But Miss Lamb frowned sternly at their inattention. They sighed deep, full-bellied sighs, and opened their books.

The governess's plans for lessons as usual were upset, however, although not by Clementine or Edwin. Grandpa Tipton came charging into the schoolroom and announced, "I've come to say goodby!"

He really was leaving, then, as he had threatened.

"Can't stomach it!" he said. "From now until the fair opens it'll be just unbearable. All this royalty nonsense sticks in my craw. Beggin' your pardon, Lambie; I know you've got a queen over there in England, and it's perfectly all right for you to curtsy and carry on. But I can't and I won't, either. I'm going back to my little house for some peace and quiet."

Clementine and Edwin begged him to change his mind, but he was firm.

"No, I've got to go now before they have me up on the fitting table in a pair of velvet knee britches. Your ma's a gentle little thing, Clem, but once she's made up her mind, she sweeps everything in her way. Keep up the good fight, Miss Lambie-O," he added. "Don't let them make this grandchild of mine into one of those spineless, niminy-piminy society girls. See that she grows into a real person, a real live woman, and I'll be everlastingly grateful to you."

He hugged the children and shook Miss Lamb's hand heartily. Then he hurried to the nursery for a look at the little ones. They heard him thump down the stairs, the front door slammed, and he was gone.

After that, even Miss Lamb couldn't keep them at their work. She soon gave up and said, "It's a beautiful day. We'll go for a walk and do our French on the way. Maybe after you've had an airing you'll be able to study. Get your hats and coats."

It was more like a run than a walk. The brisk spring breeze blew them along and they were all so busy hanging onto their hats that French was forgotten for the moment.

"Good riddance," thought Clementine. "Let it all blow away and I won't care. Let everything blow away."

Chapter Eleven

*A*fter *several days* of frantic activity in the sewing room, Aunt Maude decided that her gowns were far enough along, and that she must go home to Pittsburgh. She was leaving all the plans in her darling sister's hands, and would see to outfitting her boys and her husband with their local tailor.

"Then we'll all be back in time for the Emperor's visit and the opening day and all the excitement. Come, Edwin love, get your things packed, and Nanny, please get the baby ready."

Edwin set up a howl. "Ow! Ow!" he yelled, as if he had sat on a pin. The noise startled Nathaniel and Adelaide and they howled, too. Clementine saw her chance, and pushing back her luncheon plate, she added her voice to the din. In vain the nannies tried to get them all quieted.

"Let Edwin stay! Please, please, Aunt Maude; it's only a month! Let him stay!" And Edwin shrilled, "I don't want to go back to Pittsburgh yet. I want to stay here with my cousin."

Poor Aunt Maude held her ears and turned help-lessly to her sister.

"Why not, Maude? After all, it is only a month, and Clementine and Edwin are so fond of each other and; play so well together — " Here Clementine kicked Edwin under the table. He howled again, and this time it was real.

"But what about his lessons? His Latin — "

"Hush that noise this instant," Miss Lamb ordered, and Clementine and Edwin hushed immediately. "If you like, Mrs. Peabody, I would be happy to hear Edwin's Latin lessons. We can catch up on all he's missed."

. "See, Maude, it's so simple. Leave Edwin with us. He'll be no trouble at all." Here Edwin reached out to kick Clementine, but she had pulled her legs well back under her chair and he hit only the table leg.

"And Miss Lamb can review a little easy Latin just so he won't forget everything."

"I'll be pleased to give him as much Latin as he can take," Miss Lamb answered crisply, and Edwin shud-dered and wondered if it was too late to change his mind. But his mother was convinced, and so it was de-cided. The next day Mrs. Peabody and Nanny Fergu-son and Nathaniel were off in a confusion of kisses and goodbys and last-minute directions about fans and gloves and ribbons.

And then the big house settled back into a routine that was anything but routine. Mrs. Pat was called in to sew full-time, and Sheila took over her mending chores at night. The menu for the Emperor's dinner was drawn up, and Cook and Simpson made plans for all that had to be done. The house had already had its annual spring cleaning, but Simpson decided that it must all be gone over again. All day long the maids ran up and down the backstairs with pails of hot water, with mops and dusters and lemon oil. The usual polishing of brass and copper and silver and glass went on at a frenzied rate.

Mama had decided that only handwritten invitations would do, so hour after hour when she was not in the sewing room, she sat at her desk and worked. Miss Lamb wrote a beautiful precise hand and she was pressed into service, too. Each evening after dinner she wrote invitations instead of reading aloud as she usually did. The children missed the stories — they were halfway through *David Copperfield* — and they missed her company. Nanny and Titus and Adelaide kept strictly to their established schedule, but Clementine and Edwin felt left out and neglected. They missed Grandpa Tipton, too. They hadn't realized how much difference his hearty laugh and his roars of disapproval had made in their staid household.

They found they had time on their hands for the first time since Miss Lamb had come. She was as strict as ever during lessons, and insisted they keep their minds on their work. But though she gave them hard assignments that should have kept them out of mischief, she had volunteered to help with the frantic sewing and she brought to the schoolroom yards of ruffling to be hemmed. While she stitched away at her desk, Clementine and Edwin muttered over their sums and their Latin.

Miss Lamb had discovered that Edwin's study of that ancient language had been extremely spotty. Shocked, she decided that he should begin again at the very beginning for a quick review of all he should have learned. And since he would be starting again, she also decided that Clementine would start, too.

"For," she explained, "Latin will stretch your mind and expand your vision."

Clementine felt that her mind was stretched far enough already, but Miss Lamb was firm. She didn't ask Mrs. Tipton's permission to change Clementine's studies — "Mrs. Tipton is so busy right now — " but went right ahead just as she pleased.

Clementine was surprised to find that she enjoyed the extra work. She was determined not to let Edwin outdistance her, and she studied harder than she had ever done before. Yet for all the work, she and Edwin were able to take advantage of everyone's preoccupation, and when Miss Lamb was busy in the sewing room they slipped down the backstairs to the kitchen.

They found Mrs. Culligan in her glory. Since the whole household seemed to be pivoting around the dinner for the Emperor, Mrs. Culligan was at the very heart of things. For no matter how carefully everything was arranged, if the cooking were not superb, nothing else would matter. The menu was to be long and elaborate.

"Fit for a king," Cook declared. "Fit for more'n a king. A nemperor is more'n a king, isn't he, lovey? We'll make this dinner fit for all the saints in heaven, should they decide to drop in."

Every day she practiced one of the difficult dishes she planned, and tried it out on the kitchen help.

"None of this peculiar foreign stuff with names you can't even say," she announced. "It'll be plain old American, and we'll give His Royal Emperor a treat he won't soon forget."

Whatever her feelings about foreign food, Mrs. Culligan's versions of plain old American were elaborate. She tried out ice cream with flaming bananas, delicate cakes and pies, all sorts of intricate puddings. And Clementine and Edwin made it their business to be there at tasting time.

It was in the kitchen that they heard all the news about the centennial. The battle between Cook and Pat was still raging: she was for the centennial and he was against it. Every day he quoted from articles in the *Bulletin* that criticized the handling of the centennial affairs, and he predicted daily that the whole thing would be a tremendous failure.

"A failure, is it?" Cook would roar. "Look around yez, man! There's eight of us right here who are planning to see every glorious inch of it, and we'll pay our way in, too. And there's many others who feel the same way, you'll see!"

"I'll see, all right." Pat was gloomy at the prospects. "I see it every day, with my own eyes. The buildings still not finished, and the statues still in their crates with the rain leaking in on them, and the railway tracks just about laid but the station not finished yet. Oh, I see plenty."

"Well, you blasphemous unbeliever, uncross your eyes and cast them on the paper, now. Read me what it says about His Highness."

It was from the news in the kitchen that Clementine learned there was an empress as well as an emperor of Brazil, and that both of them were coming to the fair. She hurried to pass the news on to Mama, who came close to fainting with excitement, then recovered to push the sewing even faster. It was in the kitchen, too, that she learned that the Empress had been invited officially to open the Women's Pavilion and had graciously accepted.

"Oh, dear, Papa will be in a state. He won't care for that at all."

"We'll stay out of his way, then," mumbled Edwin, his mouth full of delicate apple fritters Cook was experimenting with. It seemed like a very sensible idea.

Indeed it seemed like a good idea to stay out of everyone's way. Everywhere they went someone was sure to say, "Just step aside, Master Edwin, dear; I need to clean there," or, "Now Miss Clementine, can't you find something better to do with your time when we're all so dreadfully busy?"

It was only in the kitchen that they felt absolutely welcome. Although Mrs. Culligan roared at them to give her room to work, a moment later she was offering them a taste of something and asking, "How's that, now? Good enough to bring their highfalutin Highnesses to their knees, is it?"

It was in the kitchen that Clementine and Edwin learned about Shantyville. Pat announced, "Oh, himself is in a rare temper today. With all the art and culture and la-de-da, there is them who're getting ready for a different kind of show, and himself can't do a thing about it. They're building a Shantyville: it's goin' up just outside the fair grounds, and it's outside his jurisdiction. Oh, I tell ye, there'll be many a one who'll pay more to see a two-headed calf and a giant and a midget than to see all the statues in the world. And the belly-dancers — "

"Out of my kitchen with your foul language! Sayin' that word in front of these two innercents — " Mrs. Culligan grabbed her broom and took out after him, and Pat left hastily, laughing.

"What word?" asked Clementine and Edwin together.

"Why speakin' of bellies right out in mixed company. Oh, shame to him, I say! I'll be speakin' to Mrs.

Pat about him. And you two, mind you forget it, now. I'll not have you repeating such things. The stinkin' spalpeen, that Pat!"

So they had something new to think about. A two-headed calf! And a belly-dance, whatever that might be. Sure to be interesting though, or Mrs. Culligan wouldn't have made such a fuss. But Pat had said, "pay to see them." It was the first time they had realized that the fair wouldn't be entirely free.

When they asked her, Mrs. Culligan reassured them. "Never you mind, my lovies. Mr. Horace will see that you get in to view all the grand things; don't worry your heads about it."

The art gallery and Machinery Hall and all the state buildings and the concerts, yes. But both knew there wasn't a chance that Mr. Horace would pay their way to see a two-headed calf or a belly-dancer. And all their pocket money was going to pay for the broken basket cart. They were, as Cook would have put it, in a pickle for fair. Well, they would just have to get out of their pickle, but that was easier said than done.

"How do you get money if your parents won't give it to you?" they wondered. Neither one had the answer, but they tried to think of one.

"We could beg," Clementine said excitedly. "We could tear our clothes and dirty our faces and stand on Chestnut Street and beg."

"Someone would know us and tell Uncle Horace,

and that would be the end of the fair for us. You'll have to think of something better than that."

"I don't know why I have to think of it," she grumbled. "You think, too."

"I am! I am! But nothing is happening up here!" He banged his head with his hand in despair.

They were sitting in the empty schoolroom, supposedly hard at work. They could hear rapid chatter from the sewing room, and a murmur that meant Nanny was singing to Adelaide and Titus.

Their books were open in front of them, but neither Clementine nor Edwin was reading. All they could think of was a way to earn some money. Clementine went through a list of all the things that had to be done around the house, but every chore already had someone assigned to it and doing a better job than she or Edwin could do. And then it came to her.

"Pat is always complaining that with all the coming and going he hasn't had time to clean the stable properly. We'll do it and surprise him, and he'll be so pleased he'll pay us."

It did seem like a good idea. They closed their books and, without bothering to tell anyone, they charged down the backstairs. No one noticed as they streaked out of the kitchen door and across the backyard to the stable.

"Quick, grab a pitchfork and start working," Clementine ordered.

"What do I do with it?"

"Take up this dirty straw, stupid, and then we'll put down clean. It's easy."

"It stinks in here."

"Smells," she corrected. "Miss Lamb says you mustn't use 'stinks.' "

"Well, I think it stinks and — yech! I've got my boots all mucky."

Clementine looked, and she had too. Well, it was too bad. They probably should have taken time to change. She hiked her dress up and tucked it in her waistband so that it, at least, would stay clean.

"Now we've got it all piled up here, what do we do with it?"

"We'll decide that later. Here, give me a hand with this bale of straw."

Together they broke open the bale and began to scatter the fresh straw over the stall floor. It was sneezy work. The straw blew all over and Edwin began to act silly. He pranced around, throwing the straw into the air and letting it fall wherever it blew.

"Oh, I'm to be Queen of the May, Mother, I'm to be Queen of the May," he sang, prancing and tossing. Soon they were both covered. Straw stuck in their hair and covered their clothes. It was fun and funny, and they were laughing so hard they didn't hear Mrs. Pat coming down from her rooms over the carriage house.

"What the dickens is going on here?" she shouted, and tripped over the rake that Edwin had carelessly

dropped in the doorway. "My soul to glory!" she screamed. "It's a trap you young divils has laid!" She was doing a lively jig, one foot and the other foot, trying to get her balance and not fall into the pile of straw and manure they had raked up.

Clementine and Edwin were truly horrified, but somehow they couldn't turn off their giggles immediately, and they went on laughing, even when she sprawled on the stable floor. They laughed until the tears ran down their cheeks. They tried to help plump Mrs. Pat but they couldn't get a grip on her.

"Let go! Let Go! You're making it worse! I'll get up me own self."

Finally she struggled to her feet. The last giggles ran out of them, and the two children stood silent, shocked at what they had done.

"I'm a-waitin' a reasonable answer," she said angrily. "What the divil is goin' on? And what did I iver do to the two of you, that you should treat me suchlike? And me in a clean dress about to go in the house to sew. What, pray tell, are you doin' in Pat's stable and him and the horses not here? And what will your Miss Lamb say to this, her that's supposed to bring you up clean and decent and educated, now? And who's to answer for my dirty dress and my barked shins and the damage to my liver because of the start you gave me? And, dear Saint Michael have mercy on us all, have you lost your wits altogether now?"

They couldn't get a word in edgewise against the

rush of her questions, for Mrs. Pat was a great talker. And to tell the truth, they didn't know how to answer. There was just nothing to say.

Mrs. Pat took each one by an ear, gingerly, for they were well-covered with straw, and just as they were and just as she was, led them into the kitchen, talking all the while.

Once inside the kitchen door she shouted for Simpson. He gave one look at the culprits and said, "Hush, Mrs. Pat. Whatever's happened, it's not necessary that the madam hear about it. Miss Lamb will handle it. Cook, get tea for Mrs. Pat."

He hurried upstairs to the sewing room and was down in a short time with Miss Lamb at his heels.

"What — " she gasped.

Mrs. Pat, refreshed by her quick swig of strong tea, began to pour out the story all over again. Mrs. Culligan was inclined to sympathize with the children, and she added her opinion to the uproar. When she could finally make herself heard, Miss Lamb said in her brisk, clipped way, "That will do, Mrs. Pat. I'll take charge now. Outside, children! Clean off every piece of that straw, and scrape your boots — scrape them well, mind you! And then come to me in the schoolroom. We'll get to the bottom of this piece of mischief."

Chapter Twelve

urprisingly enough, when she heard their side of the story, Miss Lamb was sympathetic.

"You do have a tendency to go about things all wrong, both of you. But you are right; you should have a chance to earn some pocket money," she said. "It is important to one's self-esteem to learn to do a stint well and be paid for it." Just what that meant Clementine wasn't sure, but it sounded encouraging. Miss Lamb continued to think aloud. "But what can that chore be? Everything around here is already being done."

"Could we black the stove for Cook? Or shine Papa's shoes? Or deliver the laundry?"

"Henry Kelly does that. It would be wrong to deprive him of his money, for he needs it badly. No, I just can't think — Wait, I believe I've struck upon it!" She started for the sewing room next door, and Clementine and Edwin trailed after her.

Mrs. Tipton was on the fitting platform, turning slowly as Miss Pierce and her niece adjusted the hem of her ball gown. She was listening with only half an ear as Miss Lamb explained the problem.

"Gracious no, what do they need money for? Mr. Tipton provides for all their needs, and as for the fair, they'll have guest passes, of course. A little higher right here in front, don't you think, Miss Pierce? But if you insist, I suppose I could speak to Mr. Tipton and ask him to restore their pocket money. They needn't go on paying for that dreadful basket cart any longer."

Miss Lamb disagreed and said so. The broken cart was the children's responsibility and they should learn to accept responsibility. She even said that Lady Alice felt that a few small responsibilities developed character in children.

"Well, in that case — although I do think it a bit strange. Perhaps English children need more character, do you suppose? Anyway, they may have some little chore as long as they don't cause trouble. Longer there, Miss Pierce, a whole inch, I would say. We are so dreadfully busy, you know."

So Clementine and Edwin were given jobs in the sewing room for which they would be paid twenty-five cents a week. Each day for an hour Edwin was to pick up all the threads and ravelings from the sewing-room carpet, and stick all the many scattered pins back into their pincushions. Clementine would have preferred his assignment, for she was to hem yards of ruffling with tiny neat stitches. But the hour went by somehow, and twenty-five whole cents every single week made it worthwhile.

Pleased as they were about the arrangements, there were times when the day went by very slowly. Spring was calling outside, and the children heard it. A new party dress for Clementine was in progress, and as she tried to stand motionless while she was fitted, she could see the green trees outside and a patch of bright blue sky. The fittings took forever. Mama and Miss Pierce were perfectionists, and not until every seam was exactly right was Clementine allowed to move. It was going to be a very pretty dress — pink silk with tiny tucks and rows of lace drawn back over a wine and pink striped underskirt. Miss Pierce said it was the new fishwife style that was all the rage abroad.

"Fishwife!" snorted Edwin. "Why would anyone want to go to a party looking like a fishwife? And why would they want to go to a party anyway?"

"Don't be cheeky, Edwin," answered Mama. "If there is a fishwife style for young gentlemen, we'll have one made for you."

Miss Pierce hurried to get out her latest fashion magazine from abroad, and sure enough, little boys were wearing a variation of the same thing — a striped overblouse and a pointed striped hat like those of a French fisherman. Edwin shuddered and was absolutely quiet for the rest of the hour while the talk of fashions swirled around him, and Clementine did her best to stand still and get the horrible fitting over.

"Pink stockings and slippers, or maybe pale lavender boots with scalloped sides?" Mama couldn't decide. "We'll shop for them right away. You'll be quite presentable, dear, if only you remember to keep your stockings straight and that mop of hair under control. And remember your manners and your curtsies. Oh, dear, if you'll only make an attempt to live up to this beautiful dress. And stand still! It is not necessary to wiggle around!"

The children were feeling very housebound and shut-in, and they needed a good run. So did Miss Lamb, apparently, for she was heard to sigh a lot and look longingly out the window as she sewed or helped them with their lessons.

Finally one day she announced that she would have to take her Thursday afternoon off. Mrs. Tipton raised her eyebrows rather disapprovingly. In her mind, nothing should come before the important business of getting ready for the Emperor and Empress. But Miss Lamb had made up her mind.

"There is an errand that I must do," she said, and that was that.

"We'll go along with you," Clementine said privately to her governess. "Our lessons are done, and our sewing-room stint is done for the day. If we don't get out, we'll bust."

"Burst," said Miss Lamb.

"No, we'll bust — with a big explosion all over the place. Please, you know we need the exercise. We'll go wherever you go and not be a bother, we promise."

"Dear, it's not that you'll be a bother. It's just — I cannot take you along. I cannot. I wouldn't dare."

"You're going to another meeting," Clementine guessed shrewdly. "I saw the sign the other day. It's a women's rights meeting, and we aren't supposed to know about it."

Miss Lamb tilted her firm little chin in the air and said, "What I do with my own time is my own business. I only promised not to espouse the women's rights cause publicly. There is a side door to the meetinghouse, so I won't be going in publicly."

"Well, I only hope Papa doesn't hear about it," Clementine said. She had no intention of telling, and Miss Lamb knew her well enough to understand that. She laughed, but finally said, "All right, you may come along as far as the square if you'll promise me that you won't take one step beyond it. Take your hoops and you'll be able to get some exercise, but no impulsive notions, now. Just plain hoop-rolling and deep breathing."

Edwin and Clementine were so pleased to get away from the routine of the schoolroom and the sewing room that they were willing to promise anything. They tagged along eagerly, first running ahead of Miss Lamb and then following on her heels. All three felt as if they had been released from prison.

When they got to the house on Rittenhouse Square where the meeting was to be held, they found a number of ladies going in the front door. Some arrived in carriages, some came on foot. The women's rights meeting had attracted quite a crowd.

A young man was there, saying politely to each newly-arrived lady, "Hawkins of the *Public Ledger,* ma'am. Would you be so kind — Just a word, ma'am, how you feel about — No offense meant, madam, just trying to gather some news — Hawkins of the *Public Ledger* — You don't have to give your name, madam, just an opinion — "

Each time he was rebuffed. The ladies hurried up the front steps and into the house. Miss Lamb took advantage of the commotion to slip in through the garden gate to the side door. The children didn't even realize she was gone until they turned and found that she was no longer standing beside them.

Mr. Hawkins of the *Public Ledger* sighed, put his hat back on his head, and stowed his notebook in his pocket. "Never saw a bunch of women who had absolutely nothing to say." He sounded very discouraged. "I've tried ten times to get in the door and each time I've been turned away. Politely, I'll admit; it was all very genteel, but I got thrown out just the same."

Clementine and Edwin were sympathetic.

"Nobody grownup ever tells you anything," Clementine said. "At least, never anything you want to hear."

"All I want is a few words about the women's movement — something that will help people make up their minds fairly, that's all. But they won't even tell me what they are hoping to gain." He sighed again. "My editor's not going to be happy about this," he said sadly. Then he brightened. "How would you two like to give me an interview? 'According to a well-dressed lady and gentleman strolling around Rittenhouse Square — I won't mention the hoops."

They giggled. Mr. Hawkins was able to be funny even when he was discouraged. Clementine liked that. She liked the shock of curly red hair that seemed to be as unmanageable as her own, and his blue eyes with little laugh lines running out from the corners.

"We're supposed to be rolling our hoops and breathing fresh air while we wait for our governess," she volunteered. "I don't think she'd want us mentioned in the newspapers."

"Your governess? Is she in there, too? Would she make a statement, do you think? Could you persuade her? I don't dare go back to my editor empty-handed. Could you save my life?"

For an instant Nanny's stock warning about petting mad dogs and speaking to strangers went through Clementine's mind. Only for an instant. Right on the heels of that thought hurried another: this Mr. Hawkins certainly wasn't a mad dog and he didn't seem a bit like a stranger. So she said, "We could ask. But Miss Lamb doesn't always do what we ask; she does what she thinks is right. So you shouldn't count on it."

"I won't count on a thing," he said. "If you'll just ask, I'll be eternally grateful."

"Clem," warned Edwin, "Miss Lamb won't like this. She'll be hopping mad."

"Oh, hush, Edwin, I'll take that chance. Come on, we'll roll our hoops and breathe and keep an eye out. As soon as the meeting is over we'll ask Miss Lamb. We'll see you later, Mr. Hawkins."

They made the sedate tour of the square time after time. Edwin kept prophesying gloom and doom and even said, "You talk about the crazy ideas I get! You think of worse ideas in one minute than I could come up with in an hour."

"Edwin Peabody," she said, "you are nothing but a lily-livered milksop who couldn't say boo to a goose!" This was one of Cook's favorite phrases, and Edwin had no answer.

Around and around they went, always keeping an eye on the brownstone house where the meeting was taking place. They breathed in the fresh air and whacked their hoops as commanded, but their hearts were not really in it. Each time they passed Mr. Hawkins they waved cordially and he waved back from his post by the side gate.

At the first sign of activity at the front door, they slung their hoops over their shoulders and raced across to take up their watch. Many ladies streamed out the front door and down the front steps, talking excitedly, but Miss Lamb was not among them. The children did not expect her to be. They watched the side gate, and in a moment it clicked quietly and Miss Lamb slipped out. Clementine and Edwin each clutched at a hand.

"Goodness," she exclaimed. "Did you miss me that much? I wasn't gone long."

"Miss Lamb, this is our friend Mr. Hawkins from the newspaper andhewouldliketoaskyouaboutthemeeting — "

Just as Edwin had predicted, Miss Lamb was angry. Dignified, ladylike, but definitely angry.

"I do not know the gentleman," she said icily. "Come, children, we never speak to strangers."

She started to walk on, but Clementine boldly blocked her way. "I don't think that's right, Miss Lamb. He only wants to ask about the meeting and what it's all about so people can make up their minds fairly. And Mr. Hawkins isn't a stranger. We've become friends, and he's a very nice person."

Miss Lamb looked up at the tall young man. It was a long, appraising look that seemed to go right through him. Evidently she did not dislike what she saw for her voice was a trifle less cold as she said, "You have apparently charmed my young charges, sir. What do you hope to gain?"

"I hope for a short interview, miss. You needn't give any names; just a few words about the meeting that took place, and what was said, and — "

"So you can make a joke of it in your newspaper and

142

hold us women up to scorn? No, thank you, Mr. Hawkins! The press has had its fun at the expense of the women's movement. We have decided that we will encourage no articles except by female writers who will treat our cause honorably. Good day, sir." She nodded politely but firmly and started to move on.

"But you misunderstand me, miss. My intentions are entirely honorable. And surely it's not my fault that I'm not a woman reporter, now, is it? There's no way I can change that. Come now, I'm prepared to be fair. Can't you be as fair to me?"

She did not answer, and he said eagerly, "How's this for a bargain? I'll let you read my article before I turn it in, and if it displeases you in any way I'll tear it up right before your eyes. What could be fairer than that? And if you convince me, don't you see how many readers you'll reach, and convince them too?"

Miss Lamb wavered. "Well, since you put it that way —"

"And your name needn't be used at all, if you prefer; just your opinions."

"Oh, I do definitely prefer. In fact, I insist. I forbid you to use it, sir. It would mean the loss of my position."

"Then I'll not even ask, just to make you feel free to speak. Now, where can we talk?" the young man asked. "May I treat you all to an ice at the confectioner's on Chestnut Street?"

Miss Lamb usually frowned on ices as being bad for

one's health, but before she had time to refuse, Mr. Hawkins had the little group turned in the direction of Chestnut Street and the sweets shop. He hurried them along for fear Miss Lamb might change her mind, and they all had to trot to keep up with his long, loping strides.

Once in the shop, seated at a round table and served with raspberry ices, Clementine and Edwin swung their feet happily and spooned up their treat in tiny bites to make it last longer. The luscious frost melted on their tongues and slid gently down their throats. Mr. Hawkins and Miss Lamb were neglecting their ices shamefully. Deep in conversation, they didn't seem to notice that the pink confections in front of them were melting away. Mr. Hawkins scribbled furiously in his notebook as Miss Lamb talked.

She told him what the women's movement was really about, not the ridiculous things that cartoonists and writers made fun of — smoking cigars and chewing tobacco and wearing mannish clothes. She spoke of what they hoped to gain for all women everywhere, how important it was that women be allowed to vote, to receive equal pay for equal work, to own property in their own names, and many other goals. She listed her arguments in the clear and organized manner she used in teaching, and it was very convincing.

Mr. Hawkins kept saying, "Wonderful! Wonderful!" as he wrote.

At the very end of her explanation she finished by

144

talking about the Women's Pavilion at the Centennial Exposition and how it would sum up all the contributions women had made in the past and what they hoped to achieve in the future. It would show that indeed there was no end to the work that women were capable of performing, and to the great things they could add to what was being done in the world. And then, at last, she stopped for breath.

"A great finish!" Mr. Hawkins said. "I won't have to change a word — we can use this just as you've told it to me. It's only a shame you don't want the credit for it. Read it, if you can decipher my scribbles, and if you approve I'll get it in the next edition. I'll bring you a copy, fresh off the press — " He stopped, then added, "But I don't know where you live and I promised not to ask."

The unpredictable Miss Lamb, who up to now had been so very predictable, smiled.

"And you haven't asked, Mr. Hawkins. You've been as good as your word. But I didn't promise not to give it to you, did I?" She took a card from her purse and wrote on it, rose quickly, bowed to her new friend and said, "Come, children." By the time Mr. Hawkins had untangled his long legs and stood up, she was shepherding her charges out the door.

She had little to say on the way home, and seemed occupied with her thoughts. As they went up the front steps she said very sternly, "This doesn't change our rule, you understand. We never, never speak to strangers."

"Or pet mad dogs," added Clementine with a giggle.

Chapter Thirteen

ust as he had promised, Mr. Hawkins brought the newspaper article. Miss Lamb was teaching at the time, Simpson told him, and could not be disturbed, so he left the plain brown envelope to be delivered to her later. He called again, and this time she was free for a moment of conversation. She returned to the schoolroom, pink-cheeked and smiling. If the children thought they could be inquisitive about her visitor, they were wrong. She disciplined them both for their sauciness with twenty extra lines of Latin.

Simpson smiled knowingly at her after that, but the rest of the household did not notice that Miss Lamb had a steady gentleman caller. A whole troop of gentlemen callers could have come and gone and no one would have noticed, they were so busy.

The article in the *Public Ledger* was noticed, however. Papa read everything in every newspaper about the centennial before he finished his breakfast, and this particular article called forth much angry humphing and grumphing and snorts. Mr. Hawkins had not converted Papa, at any rate, but perhaps there were others who had second thoughts about the cause of women.

The activity in the house had risen to an absolute frenzy. Cook and Mama had decided on the final revision of the menu, and Mrs. Culligan ran through it once for practice. Everyone, upstairs and downstairs, pronounced it perfect. The rehearsal was such a festive affair that Mama even invited Miss Lamb and Clementine and Edwin to dine downstairs, while Nanny was served some of everything in the nursery.

The invitations had gone out, forty-eight for dinner and an extra two hundred and fifty guests to come later for the reception. The replies had come back with astonishing promptness. Everyone wanted a chance to meet the Emperor and Empress of Brazil.

Papa and Mama had, of course, invited President and Mrs. Grant to attend. They received a cordial reply from Mrs. Grant saying that, because of the President's recent ill health, they would come to Philadelphia very quietly and leave as soon as the opening ceremony was over, and could not partake of any of the attendant festivities.

Papa was disappointed, but the note on heavy White House stationery was quite impressive, and he handed it around for everyone to see. Mama felt that perhaps it was better, under the circumstances. One pair of celebrities would be quite enough.

Old Mr. Lowndes was hounded to make his flowers come into bloom at exactly the right time. He grumbled that only a fool would expect to hurry nature, but nevertheless he sprayed and misted and picked and pruned until the conservatory was in a state of perfection that outdid even his usual high standards. Bushels of flowers would be ordered in, of course, to fill vases all over the house. But in addition, Mama wanted the conservatory softly lighted with candelabra to invite strolls in the perfumed air.

The work in the sewing room was finished at last. The gowns were pressed and stuffed with tissue paper and hanging in every available wardrobe and closet. Some even hung in the schoolroom, covered with dust covers. Miss Pierce and her niece had taken their sewing machine and left. Clementine and Edwin had each earned several twenty-five-cent pieces. They hoarded them against the great day when they would be needed.

They read the newspapers as avidly as Papa did, both the respectable *Public Ledger* and the *Bulletin*, and also downstairs in the kitchen they read Cook's racy *Police Gazette*. The newspapers were full of nothing else but the Centennial Exposition and its marvels — that is, if it ever opened at all. Last-minute construction was still going on and last-minute exhibitions were arriving from all over the world. There were those who felt that it was going to be the most magnificent fair ever to be held. There were just as many who predicted it would be a failure on such a scale as the world had never seen. Everyone was vio-

lently for or against it. No one, it seemed, was in-between.

But as the day drew closer, public opinion gradually shifted to all-out approval of the scheme, and to the belief that it would be all everyone had hoped for and much, much more.

Papa was in a constant uproar. He had turned his business over to trusted subordinates and was devoting all his time to seeing that the fair would open as planned. His good friend Mr. Wanamaker was in charge of the arrangements for the grand opening. The two men had endless conferences about seating arrangements for the dignitaries who would be coming from all over the country and, indeed, representing all the world. There would be ambassadors from all the countries with exhibits in the show, and it was up to Papa and Mr. Wanamaker to arrange for their national anthems to be played as they entered, and their flags to be displayed.

Members of the press were clamoring for tickets. Seats had to be arranged where these reporters could see and hear everything and send the good news back to their home towns.

There were demands from elected politicians and from those who hoped to be elected, from leaders in every field. The members of the women's committee, all seven hundred and fifty of them, with silver stars glittering on their white dresses, were to sit on the platform, too. They insisted on it. And of course the committee of directors and their wives were to sit on the dignitaries' platform as near as possible to the place where President and Mrs. Grant and the Emperor and his Empress would be.

On the other side, facing Memorial Hall, an inclined platform had been built in front of the Main Building. It was to hold the huge orchestra and the chorus of one thousand voices.

All in all, there was a tremendous amount of arranging to do. No wonder Papa was excited. Belowstairs in the kitchen the excitement ran quite as high. Once breakfast was over on May tenth, the great day, Papa said all the servants might have the day off to do as they pleased. Nanny, of course, would stay home with Titus and Adelaide, and walk out in the afternoon to see all the decorations in Rittenhouse Square. Mrs. Culligan decided that after the dinner and reception of the night before, her feet would never stand the strain. She would go on other and quieter fair days. Pat would be needed with the carriage, but Mrs. Pat was planning to attend with Katie Rose. The younger maids would not dream of missing the excitement, no matter how tired they were from the night before. They had young men calling for them, three policemen and a fireman from the nearby station house. And Miss Lamb had been invited by Mr. Hawkins to sit with him in the press section.

"What are you going to wear?" asked Clementine.

"Just what I already have," Miss Lamb said. "My

navy blue. But I've put red cherries and a white ribbon on my bonnet to make it festive."

Clementine was to wear red, white, and blue, too. Edwin had his best white sailor suit with navy braid and stars and a tricolor ribbon around his hat. Clementine had a slightly nautical dress of white, with red and white striped stockings and a blue straw hat. She hated the fussing that had gone into making the outfit, but she was pleased that she would go off looking so elegant.

"I'll make a special effort to behave," she promised Miss Lamb. "It isn't every day that I get invited to a one hundredth birthday party."

They, with everyone else in Philadelphia, watched the skies anxiously and tried to guess what the weather would be. It had been a long wet spring and everyone prayed for enough days of pleasant weather to dry up the mud at the fair grounds. There was still construction going on right up to the last minute.

Rumors flew wildly, and changed three times a day. First, the New Jersey building would never be finished in time! No, that was wrong, it was the New Hampshire house that was still being hammered into place. A shipment of paintings from France had been lost — no, they had been found but not uncrated. A sudden storm had broken many panes of glass at Memorial Hall! Disaster! But then the *Ledger* said they would be replaced at once.

The *Police Gazette* pushed its stories of violent

crime and dastardly deeds to the back pages and rushed into print each issue with a changing, unfounded rumor.

No one really lost heart. It was all part of the excitement of the fair.

Somehow Clementine had assumed that she and Edwin would go with her parents. Aunt Maude and Uncle Peabody and the older Peabody boys had seats very close to the dignitaries' platform. It seemed only logical that Edwin and Clementine would too.

"I hope we sit close and see everything," she said. Edwin agreed that if they got stuck way in the back and couldn't see or hear it would be a shame. Simpson assured them that with Mr. Tipton the head of the committee, they would undoubtedly have prize seats. It wasn't until a few days before the opening that Mama said, "I do hope Miss Lamb will keep a close eye on you two. Hold on to her hand, do you hear? There will be quite a crush and you don't want to get separated."

"I thought we'd be up on the platform with you and Papa."

"Gracious no! That will be no place for children, but Papa will see that you and Edwin and Miss Lamb have excellent seats in the distinguished visitors' section. He wants you to be able to remember this day all the rest of your lives."

Edwin opened his mouth to say, "But Miss Lamb is planning to go with — " when Clementine gave him a jab in the ribs that jarred it shut again. Mama hurried on about one of her many errands. When she was out of hearing, Edwin tried again.

"Miss Lamb isn't going with us. You know she's going to sit with Mr. Hawkins."

Clementine said calmly, "I know that and you know that, but Mama doesn't. Edwin, you stupid, don't you see what this means?"

"What?" he asked.

Clementine said slowly and impressively, "Edwin, this means that you and I are going to the fair by ourselves!"

"We'd never dare," he whispered.

"I dare. We'll go alone, and we'll have a time we won't forget."

"That's right," he agreed, thinking it over. "Uncle Horace wants us to remember it all the days of our lives, and we will."

It was going to take some careful planning. One word of what they intended to do and their fine day would be spoiled, and Miss Lamb's besides, for it was plain that she was looking forward with great pleasure to her day with Mr. Hawkins. It was entirely possible that none of them would be allowed out to see the fair at all if they gave away their secret. And if Miss Lamb guessed what they had in mind — they shuddered to think of it.

"We'll take advantage of the confusion," Clementine decided. "Everyone will be so excited and mixed up, and each one will think we're with someone else. We'll manage to get out without anyone noticing. It'll work; you'll see."

"It just better had," said Edwin gloomily. "Between them, Miss Lamb and Uncle Horace will chop us to mincemeat if they catch us."

Clementine remembered in time to ask about their guest passes. She didn't exactly come right out and say that Miss Lamb had sent her to get them, but the way she put it her mother got that impression.

"Miss Lamb's busy doing Latin with Edwin, Mama, and please, do you want to give me the visitor passes now so you won't have to remember them in all the confusion of May tenth?"

"A good idea. Miss Lamb is very thoughtful." Mama rummaged in her desk. "Here they are — seats right in front where you won't miss a thing. I hope Miss Lamb will keep them in a safe place. Oh, of course she will; Miss Lamb never mislays anything. Now, where did I put that list — where could I have left it?"

Mama was burrowing in her desk like a frantic squirrel, and Clementine skipped off with the precious passes safely in her pinafore pocket. Still no plan of how she and Edwin would get away to use them. She would just have to be patient. Patient and watchful. Their chance would come.

There came a time when even Simpson agreed that everything was ready. The house fairly sparkled, every doorknob shone like a round little sun. The floors were like dark mirrors, the draperies hung at the windows in perfect folds. The guest rooms were ready, just in time for Aunt Maude and her brood to descend again in a flurry of hugs and kisses.

Nanny Ferguson and Nathaniel settled into their old places in the nursery with not even a flutter, and the two nannies took up their conversation just where they had left off.

There was a great deal of squeezing, of course, even in a house as large as the Tiptons'. Clementine moved into Miss Lamb's tiny room on a cot, and more cots were set up in Edwin's room to take care of his three grown brothers. Distant but distinguished relatives from Scranton were sleeping in Clementine's room. Clementine did not like Cousins Daisy and Frederick too well. Cousin Daisy was too fat and jolly and her husband was too thin and disagreeable. But they had no children to scatter her favorite books or toys so she didn't object. Anyway, the move into Miss Lamb's room was an interesting change. Clementine was all for change and variety whenever her usual routine life allowed for it.

Other relatives, not so distinguished, were put up on the fourth floor. No one minded the discomfort at all. The important thing was to be in Philadelphia for the opening of the fair. Nothing else mattered.

Chapter Fourteen

*T*he *excitement of waiting* couldn't go on forever. It had built to an unbearable pitch, not only in the Tipton house on Spruce Street, but everywhere in Philadelphia. Houses were draped in swaths of red, white, and blue bunting, banners proclaimed *The One Hundredth Birthday.* Hardly a householder was so poor that he could not afford a flag to fly from an upstairs window. Business men gave out small flags to be stuck in lawns and window boxes, or flag pins for lapels and hatbands. Even dogs and cats and horses wore tricolor ribbons around their necks.

The city was jammed with visitors. Everyone who had a relative, however distant, in Philadelphia was inspired to make a visit. Hotels and rooming houses were packed full. There was no room anywhere, and everyone was almost on tiptoe, waiting for the sun to come up on the great day.

And then on May ninth, the day before the fair was to open, the clouds that had been building up for days

grew ominously gray. People said nervously, "It'll clear up; it'll surely clear up." Everyone was wrong. It rained and rained and rained. Hundreds of yards of red, white, and blue bunting hung limp and soaking.

Papa couldn't believe it. It was absolutely incredible that Nature would dare do such a foul trick on the great Centennial Exposition. He stormed from window to window, looking for a rift in the dark sky. There was none.

Mama was in a frenzy. With a house full of housebound guests to keep happy, and a splitting headache besides, she tried hard to smile and chat graciously, groping for her smelling salts when things were too bad. Fortunately, in the afternoon most of the ladies retired for naps, and the gentlemen gathered in the library for cigars and politics.

Lessons had been suspended for a few days, and it would have been hard to hold them anyway, with guests' trunks piled up, and ball gowns hanging in the schoolroom where they would not get mussed.

The house seemed unusually quiet after lunch, with the ladies napping and most of the gentlemen snoozing in Papa's deep leather library chairs. Adelaide and Nathaniel and Titus were all asleep, and the nannies rocked and nodded. Peter, Nesbit, and Weston Peabody, Edwin's big brothers, had gone out to see the city in spite of the rain. They had greeted Edwin and Clementine with kindly pats on the head and had asked about their school work, and then they had gone out, not saying where or suggesting that Edwin and Clementine might come along.

Miss Lamb rested on her bed and read. For her it was a quiet moment in a week of high-pitched excitement. Clementine murmured something about checking on the kitchen situation, and Miss Lamb only warned drowsily, "Don't get in the way, dears. Cook has a lot on her mind today, so don't do anything to upset her." They promised, and hurried down the backstairs to the kitchen.

Here there was no quiet moment, no naps, no rests. Every space, every table top, every shelf was in use. Desserts were cooling in the dark buttery behind the kitchen in tubs of cracked ice. Some of the wines were chilling, others were being brought to room temperature. The soup, in a pot as big as a wash boiler, was on the back of the stove, needing only rewarming in the butler's pantry upstairs before being served. Mrs. Culligan had the great roasts of beef already in the oven, and she fussed and clucked and banged the oven door between bursts of swearing and triumphant singing. The dinner, if it was the success it promised to be, would be Mrs. Culligan's triumph. She was generous enough to say she couldn't have done it half so well without all the fine help she was getting.

The dining-room doors were closed, and the long table was already being set. Lowndes said the "bought-in" flowers were a shabby lot compared to his own conservatory of home-grown ones, but he hummed as he grumbled, and banked the table with red and white roses and sprays of blue larkspur. Tricolor ribbons ran from the centerpiece to each of the forty-eight places.

The silver and crystal had been polished and repolished, yet Simpson gave each piece one more careful inspection before he allowed it to be loaded on the dumbwaiter and hauled upstairs. Katie Rose received it tenderly and set the table just so. Katie Rose and Simpson would supervise and instruct the twenty-four hired footmen in livery who were to do the actual serving. They had had a rehearsal the day before. Simpson put them through their paces until the poor fellows were ready to drop, before he said he was satisfied. Each man was exactly six-feet-two-inches tall, their uniforms were red and blue with gold braid on the coats and breeches, and brass buckles shone on their shoes.

"Now you're not to hang around and wait for anything," admonished Cook as the children came into the kitchen. "There'll be no treats, that's for sure; but never mind, you little darlin's, there'll be plenty of leftovers. You'll get your share of pretties."

It was understood that, under the circumstances, high tea would not be served. Simple trays of tea and bread and butter sandwiches would be delivered to the guests' rooms to sustain them while they dressed for dinner.

"We can help with the trays," Edwin offered. So

162

much was going on, it was unbearable to be left out of it all, to be just spectators.

"Oh, would you now, you loves? That's kind, indade," said Sheila. "I'd been wonderin' how we could get them all around in time. Here, I'll set the trays — we'll need only the small pots on each one — and do you write down the names and the rooms where we'll find people. 'Twould be a frightful thing to overlook one of the ladies."

"The gents'll have sherry in the liberry, no doubt," said Kathleen. "So that'll be easy enough. Where in God's name did you hide the sherry biscuits?"

"Nobody hid 'em, girl; it's your own stupidity has blinded you. There, in the front of the cupboard, where they belong, right under your long red nose. Now you kids run along and change, but not into your very best, mind you; we'll have no spots and stains for the grand occasion, Lord help us! Miss Lamb will see to yez, and then come right back, for it's the truth that we can use your help, and tell Miss Lamb that or she'll niver believe that you're actually wanted here."

Mrs. Culligan shouted all this after them, but most of it was wasted for they were pounding up the back-stairs to the third floor.

Miss Lamb did indeed question them. Were they sure their help was wanted? They were not bedeviling Cook for treats? Then she found stiffly starched but not quite best outfits for them both.

"When do I get to wear my pink dress?" Clementine wriggled as her hair was quickly brushed into some kind of order.

"Later, after dinner — hold still, child, or you'll never be neat enough — when you go downstairs to the reception. Wait. I'll help with the trays, too. They must be almost crazy in the kitchen with all there is to do."

The kitchen maids were both shocked and grateful that the governess was offering to carry tea trays.

"Faith presarve us, miss," said Sheila, "it'll not be proper, and what will the mistress say?"

"Pooh to proper," Miss Lamb said briskly. "The mistress'll never notice, she's so busy. Let me take the second floor trays and Clementine and Edwin can do the third and fourth floors, and we'll be done in no time."

Mrs. Culligan gave her an impulsive hug. "Oh, it's a fine girl you are, though English, and pray Heaven'll forgive you for that one mistake, it not bein' your fault at all."

"And never fear, your supper'll not be neglected," she called after them. "We'll see you're all taken care of like royalty itself, before the bigwigs even begin. And Simpson has a surprise for you besides!"

Clementine and Edwin walked carefully, balanced each small tray with care, and spilled not a drop. A knock on the door, a bow or curtsy, and it was all over in a few trips. They retired to the nursery glowing

164

with feelings of pride in their cleverness and generosity.

Peter and Nesbit and Weston poked their heads in the nursery door with a breezy greeting to the nannies. Weston tossed Titus up in the air and patted Edwin and Clementine on their heads again as if they were no older than the babies.

"Will you stay for tea here?" asked Nanny McGregor. They all laughed. "We're a bit old for a nursery tea. No, thanks just the same. We're off to a restaurant and will be back for the big doings later. Enjoy your mush and milk, Edwin, old boy. Good night, all!" and off they went.

It made Clementine and Edwin feel very left out and disappointed. It seemed as if everyone in the world was going to be doing something exciting and grownup, and here they were, sitting by the nursery fire with two infants and a toddler. Miss Lamb understood their feeling. Maybe she was feeling a little of it herself.

"You couldn't pay me to go out on a night like this," she said. "It's still raining pitchforks and hammer handles, and here we are, as cozy as can be."

Edwin brightened. "Simpson promised a surprise for supper."

"And later we're to meet the Emperor and Empress, don't forget!" Considerably cheered, they built block houses for Titus and entertained Adelaide and Nathaniel with peekaboo.

Suddenly, without so much as a knock, the nursery door burst open and Simpson came in with a tray so loaded that he could hardly see over the top of it. And right behind was Grandpa Tipton!

Even Nanny McGregor hugged him, she was so delighted, and then retired to her rocker by the fire, beet red with blushing.

"Help, help!" he shouted. "You'll strangle me, you young devils! Let go, let go! I'm not as young as I used to be, you know."

"You're younger, if I may be so bold, sir," grinned Simpson. "Who else would have thought of a mad plan like this and carried it through?"

"What plan? What kind of plan?"

"Lend a hand here, sprouts, and get this table set, for I'm famished. Then I'll explain it all."

"Enjoy your supper, one and all," said Simpson. Here he winked broadly at Grandpa. "I'll have the pleasure of your company later on."

Cook had sent up a portion of every delicacy, with a heavy emphasis on desserts. Since no one was paying attention, Clementine started with dessert and nudged Edwin to do the same. But it didn't really matter. It was all wonderful.

Grandpa ate as he talked, and sometimes talked with his mouth full, and neither the nannies nor Miss Lamb scolded him.

"Well, as you know I swore I'd never come back here and bend my knee to a foreign emperor, or mor-

166

tify myself by scuttling out backward, like a crab. And having been so firm and loud about it, my pride wouldn't let me give in and make my peace with my son, Horace. So there I was, with a battle raging between my pig-headed pride and my curiosity — and if one or the other hadn't won soon, I'd have split wide open from the battle wounds." He stopped to butter another roll. "Old Culligan does have a way with her rolls," he remarked appreciatively.

"So curiosity won — " prompted Miss Lamb.

"Yes, but my stubborn pride hung on like a bulldog. Then I worked out a truce: I would come to peek at the Emperor and his lady, but I'd not let Horace crow over me. So this afternoon I presented myself at the kitchen door and Simpson smuggled me up to his bedroom, where I'll spend the night. I'll watch the doings from the upstairs hall and be at the opening of the fair tomorrow, and Horace and Olympia need never know that this old softy gave in."

He laughed heartily at his joke, but Miss Lamb was indignant. "Mr. Tipton, it's not right! You should have one of the places of honor downstairs at the dinner, and be in the receiving line and all the rest of it!"

"Oh, Lambie dear, I've had a bellyful of these formal dinners in my lifetime, and all of them together don't compare with this supper here tonight. No, let me have my fun in my own way. I'll look down on the top of the Emperor's crown from the stair landing, and Katie Rose'll slip me a glass of champagne, and I'll drink His Majesty's health with a will. And never a dull conversation with some diamond-studded dimwit, but a game of Trot the Horsey with my grandchildren."

There was no use in arguing with him. He knew exactly what he wanted to do and intended to do it.

"We're to get dressed up and meet the Emperor at the reception," said Clementine. "And the rest of the time we'll peek with you from the stairway. Mama said we didn't have to dance."

"*Have* to dance!" he roared. "We'll *want* to dance! We'll cut the buckle right up here, my lovies. There'll be so much going on below that a little extra stamping around won't be noticed. We'll jig and we'll jiggle, Miss Lambie-O and the Nannies and all the rest of us, even the babies. We'll dance the night around. Remember, it's not every day our country gets to be one hundred years old. And even less often than that do we capture an emperor!"

Chapter Fifteen

It was a lively supper. There was no rush, for the guests' carriages were only beginning to arrive as they finished their nursery meal. The rain had slackened off to a gentle drizzle, but umbrellas were necessary. Even by hanging out of an upstairs window, it wasn't possible to see more than the shining carriages and dripping horses and the tops of umbrellas. And not until the formal dinner was over would Clementine and Edwin be presented to the royal guests.

Mama had decided, sadly, that it would be a mistake to try to keep Titus up so late. No telling what he might do or say if he was sleepy and cranky. And he was too young to remember the event the way Clementine would. But it was too bad, she felt. Titus was such a handsome little boy. Even the rulers of Brazil would certainly be impressed with him. She was not so certain about Clementine.

Miss Lamb had supervised thorough baths in the afternoon, so all that was needed was a careful washing of faces and hands, and hairbrushing, of course, and then Clementine and Edwin could get dressed. Not until the very last minute, though. Miss Lamb was not planning to take any chances on spots or spills. Katie Rose had promised to tinkle the schoolroom bell when dessert was carried into the diners, and that should time it very neatly, they decided.

Clementine's dress was laid out on Miss Lamb's bed — pale pink silk, with rows and rows of tiny tucks and ruffles and satin ribbons. After a great deal of discussion and shopping around, Mama had decided against boots and in favor of pink dancing slippers with flat bows. And white stockings with delicate white embroidery up the side. There was a matching petticoat, almost as elaborate as the dress, and under that another white petticoat with a white camisole and drawers.

Miss Lamb took a long time with Clementine's ginger hair, in spite of all her squirming and complaining, and at last had it brushed and arranged. Nothing would make it lie smooth and flat, so Miss Lamb decided to control the curls as best she could, and let them fall over her forehead and around her face. The back curls she drew up high, fastened with a pink bow, and coaxed to hang properly by brushing them around her finger.

For a minute or two it was perfect, but then Clementine tossed her head and some of the careful curls sprang out of place. There was no real hope for a fashionable hairdo, but Grandpa said it was all a pack of nonsense, anyway.

"Let her curls fly where they will," he advised. "She looks fine. That bright little face will charm the Emperor even if the curls don't. I'd like to see all that danged mop cut off short like a boy's. How'd that suit you, my little tomboy?"

The nannies were shocked. "Oh, sir," said Nanny McGregor, "you mustn't encourage her wildness, not even as a joke. Clementine must grow up to be a perfect lady."

Grandpa Tipton only chuckled.

"There are very few 'perfect' anythings, and a 'perfect lady' is the last thing I'd want for a granddaughter. Be a fine woman, my dear, and that'll be perfect enough for me. And now I must get duked out in my best, too. You can't even peek at royalty in your old clothes, you know."

Edwin was no problem at all. His fair hair hung straight and shining with only a few brush stokes, and his dark blue velvet suit was elegant. He fussed a bit about the ruffled lavender shirt, but under the circumstances he knew a few ruffles were mandatory.

The street below had been very quiet all during the dinner, but now more and more carriages were arriving, leaving their passengers and clattering away. The dinner was over and the reception would soon begin. It was at this point that Clementine and Edwin would be quietly presented, before the long formal reception line was formed. Katie Rose gave the second signal and the two children started down the stairs. Grandpa and Miss Lamb followed as far as the top of the stairs, and then hung back in the shadows where they could see, they hoped, but not be seen.

"If I fall down the steps, I'll die," whispered Clementine.

"If you do, I'll die laughing," said Edwin. His callousness made her so mad she forgot to be scared, and by the time they reached the bottom of the stairs she was smiling serenely.

Mama took them by the hand and led them forward to the place where a pleasant bearded man and a smiling lady were waiting. They couldn't be the Emperor and Empress! They looked just like anyone else at the party — not regal or royal or frightening at all. There was only time for a quick glance, time to notice that the Emperor was stout, with a blondish, reddish beard that seemed sort of pink in the light of the glistening chandelier. And that his Empress had big, big brown eyes and wore no jewels at all.

Then Clementine swooped into her deepest curtsy and Edwin was bowing, and the Empress said, in a soft accented voice, "What veree lovelee children; you must be so proud."

Aunt Maude swept them away before they could spoil the good impression they had made, the royal visitors turned away to stand in the receiving line that was forming, more guests arrived — and that was that. It was all over.

They scooted unnoticed through the dining room, empty now, and through to the butler's pantry where Simpson and Katie Rose leaned exhausted against the cupboard.

"I tried to watch ye, loves, but you was out of me line of view," said Katie. "We did fine," answered Clementine, "but I'm glad it's done with. Now we can go upstairs and watch."

"We'll all drink to your success down in the kitchen as soon as we regain our equilibrium. And tell Mr. Titus we'll endeavor to provide him with some champagne as soon as it is possible." Simpson beamed at them as they went up the backstairs to join Grandpa and Miss Lamb and the nannies in the hall. Miss Lamb hugged them both and assured them she was proud enough to burst. "Your curtsy was perfect, and your bow — Children, you were magnificent!"

"We got a grand view of the two of you," said Grandpa, "but damned if I could get a glimpse of the royalty! Maude's bustle stuck out so far it cut me off. Wearing a crown, was he? And decorated like a Christmas tree, I'll warrant."

"Not a bit of a crown, Grandpa! And his suit was plainer than Papa's! And the Empress wore cream-colored silk and a cameo around her neck on a little ribbon. Not a diamond anywhere! She said we were lovely children."

"Then she's a perfect lady, even without diamonds," declared Nanny McGregor. Nanny Ferguson agreed.

"She knows good bringing-up when she sees it, even if she is a foreigner."

From their vantage point at the top of the long stairway they could see most of the receiving line — the various members of the centennial committee and their wives, and Aunt Maude and Uncle Peabody. A palm tree interfered with their view of the entire line, but they knew that Mama and Papa were at the head of it, introducing the newly arrived guests to Dom Pedro and his wife.

The huge foyer was soon full, and guests spilled into the drawing room, the parlors, the conservatory. A mixture of scents floated up — the fragrance of all the huge bouquets and each lady's French perfume. Each guest spoke in a low refined voice, but altogether it made a din that was deafening. The string orchestra playing from behind a group of palms could hardly be heard.

It was much like looking through a kaleidoscope, where the brilliant pieces of glass fell into patterns that swirled and changed into other patterns over and over. After all two hundred and fifty of the reception guests had arrived and had paid their respects to the royalty, the patterns shifted still more.

Clementine saw Mama now and again, moving about speaking to guests, looking too beautiful to be real. After making up her mind a number of times and changing it again, she had finally decided on a gown of pale peach. Ribbons of a deeper peach color edged the yards of pleated ruffles and were wound through the heavy loops of her honey-colored hair. Grandmother Tipton's rare pink pearls glowed against her skin, for the gown was bare shouldered and low cut. The finest camelias Lowndes could grow were tucked into the curls on the top of her head and tied with a ribbon, and more ribbons cascaded down her back. She carried a fan of carved ivory and lace — indeed most of the ladies were fanning, for the crush of guests and the wet spring evening made it very warm inside. A diamond brooch flashed on her breast and the diamond bracelets that were a centennial present from Papa twinkled as she fanned.

She was beautiful, indeed, but Aunt Maude was not one bit less so. Edwin's mother wore white lace with pink silk roses tumbling down the back and catching up flounces of the lace to reveal panels of embroidered satin underneath. Her jewels were rubies from India, a necklace and earrings.

Against the sober black and white of the tail-coated gentlemen, the colors, brilliant or pale, that the ladies wore glittered and shone. For a while it was fascinating to watch. But after that little while was over, it was just more of the same thing. The voices melted together in a general clatter and it was impossible to know what anyone was saying. Nanny Ferguson and Nanny McGregor retired to their rockers in the day nursery where they could hear if the little ones stirred or cried. Miss Lamb decided to join them. After all, a party to which you are not invited is not all that interesting.

The kitchen help would be in a festive mood, she knew, but still knee-deep in work. There was to be a light buffet later on in the evening, and the dining room had to be made ready again. So Miss Lamb said the children might watch a few minutes longer, if Mr. Tipton would keep an eye on them, and she took her sewing and joined the nannies.

Perhaps if she had not been so tired she might have reconsidered, but it had been a long wearing day, and an even more wearing day was to follow. At any rate, trusting that they would soon be bored and ready for bed, she left Clementine and Edwin in Grandpa Tipton's charge.

Immediately the old man said, "Where's Katie Rose and my champagne, I wonder? My throat's dry as a bone. And I could do with one of your father's good cigars, too. I should have laid in a supply before I came up."

"We'll find Katie — "

"I know where the cigars are — " said Clementine and Edwin, speaking together. "Wait here for us, Grandpa; we'll see that you are taken care of."

"Not a chance. Not a bloomin' chance. I said I'd keep my eye on you two and I will, every minute. We'll all find Katie Rose and the cigars, and maybe a little innocent amusement besides."

They slipped down the backstairs into the butler's

pantry. The twenty-four identical footmen went in and out, not all at once, of course, replenishing their silver trays of champagne glasses. Katie Rose was there, scolding one of them.

"You, there," she said, "watch your tray, carry it straight. Not you, stupid, the tall one! Oh, holy Jesus, Mary, and Joseph, you're all tall! Go on, then, carry 'em any way you choose, but if you spill so much as a drop I'll — " The footman left and she sank down on a stool, too exasperated to even think what she would do to him.

"This evening'll be the death of me, Mr. Tipton. Promise me ye'll come to my wake and drink a toast and say a prayer for me. I've a bit put aside so when I'm laid out it'll be a jolly occasion."

"You'll make it, Katie Rose. Your wake's a lot further off than mine. Sit for a minute and we'll drink a toast to the two of us dancing many a jig in the future."

Grandpa poured a glass for Katie Rose and one for himself and they clinked glasses solemnly.

"Now look at that!" she said. "We're forgetting of the dear children. There's plain grape juice right here in the cupboard. But drink it carefully — don't spill it on your lovely clothes or leave a purple mustache. 'Twould never do at such a grand affair. And some little cakes, too. Eat up. It's a night for celebration."

"There, you see," said Grandpa. "Only a minute

ago you were planning your funeral. Have another glass, Katie, and we'll plan your wedding."

"Go along with you, sir; you've always been a tease. Why, here's Mr. Simpson. We'll plan for his wedding, for it's high time someone caught him."

Simpson came up from the kitchen at the same time that Miss Lamb came flying down from the third floor.

"You rang for me, Mr. Simpson? Is anything wrong?" She looked around to see Grandpa Tipton and her two charges and smiled with relief.

"Forgive my ring, miss. I just couldn't climb those stairs once more tonight. Nothing's wrong; don't be alarmed. In fact, it is something rather pleasant. You have a visitor downstairs."

"Me? A visitor?"

"Your Mr. Hawkins, Miss Lamb. I took the liberty of asking him in."

"Mr. Hawkins! Why — why — " she blushed and stammered and straightened her lace collar. Then she paused and asked almost fearfully, "Mr. Simpson, does Mr. Hawkins appear to you to be using our acquaintance as an excuse to get news of this dinner for his paper?"

"Miss Lamb, he appears to me to be a nice young man who'd like very much to be invited to the party that will be going on below. So I invited him in. Go on, go on," he said, giving her a gentle push. "Don't keep him waiting, or Sheila will grab him off."

She smiled radiantly and ran down the steps to the kitchen. Simpson and Grandpa Tipton sighed. "If either of us was fifty years younger, Simpson, we'd give Mr. Hawkins a run for his money. She's a fine girl. Oh, no, you don't," he said to Clementine and Edwin who were starting for the stairs. "You'll stay right by me and let Miss Lamb have her little fling by herself. We're after cigars, remember?"

"They're in the library, sir. The master keeps his best ones in the leather box. Now make sure he doesn't see you. I'd go myself, but I've got to stay right here."

"No need to worry, no need at all, Katie. We'll take our cigars and go upstairs and Mr. Horace'll never know I'm around. The library's a safe enough place. I'll wager there won't be anyone reading much this evening."

They peered out the door. The big hall was full, but there was not a relative in sight. A few quick steps, threading their way through the beautiful languid ladies and the handsome gentlemen, and they were safely in the quiet library with the door shut behind them.

The black leather humidor was on a shelf behind Papa's desk. Grandpa selected a handful and sniffed them appreciatively. "I'll say one thing for Horace — he knows a good cigar. Pity he doesn't know as much about some other things."

The door opened and closed again quickly as a

portly little man dashed in. He looked startled and guilty as he saw Grandpa and the children standing there.

"I found myself needing a small rest — " he said apologetically.

"Come in. Sit down." Grandpa Tipton was cordial. "Can't blame a fellow for wanting to get away from the crush out there. Isn't it awful? Here, light up a good cigar and put your feet up. You can hide out here as long as you like, and escape all that nonsense."

"Nonsense, sir?"

"Stupid nonsense, I call it! All that bowing and scraping and carrying on, just because the fellow's an emperor. He's no more'n a human being, isn't he? Puts his trousers on one leg at a time just like the rest of us, doesn't he? I haven't had a look at him yet, but I haven't missed much, I suspect. A crown on the head's not worth a plugged nickel if the head under it is full of pillow fluff — "

Clementine clutched Grandpa's elbow and Edwin gripped his coattail, but the champagne had made Grandpa talkative. He ignored their frantic jerks.

"Grandpa, Grandpa," Clementine said urgently. He looked down at her and patted her curls. "I'll wager there's more brains in my little granddaughter's head than in both of their majesties' together. I'd like to know the man, not the majesty, and make up my mind. I'd like to meet him man to man and talk things over and forget the bowing and scraping. Find out what's on his mind, and how he runs his country, and what he likes to read, and shake his hand like an equal."

"If this child is your granddaughter, then you must be— "

"Titus Tipton, sir, father of Horace Tipton, who's the host of this grand shebang. And your name, sir?"

The portly bearded man put out his hand and shook Grandpa's heartily, but before he could answer the door opened. The Empress stood there in the doorway and said pleadingly, "Dom Pedro, the guests are asking for you. Eet ees not polite that you should run away and hide. Come now, my dearest. There are many more who want to speak with you. His feet, they grow so very weary," she said apologetically to Grandpa.

The little man sighed and stubbed out his cigar.

"Too bad," he said. "Just as I was about to become acquainted with a friend."

He stood up, straightened his tail coat and bowed. Then the Empress took her husband and led him back to the party.

Chapter Sixteen

It was still raining when Simpson woke at five on the morning of May tenth. Grandpa Tipton was still sleeping soundly on his side of the bed and Simpson dressed in his usual silent efficient manner without disturbing him.

There was not a stir behind any of the other doors. It was not going to be easy to get the household awake and running this morning. He sighed, eased his feet into his soft slippers, and tiptoed down to the kitchen.

Mrs. Culligan was nowhere to be seen, but he could hear her. Great snorts of snores rumbled and echoed into the empty kitchen. Simpson sighed again, shook up the fire and put the. kettle on to boil. Irish tea, English tea, he set out the two pots and the cups and saucers.

The dishes had been washed the night before, at least, but nothing else had been taken care of. Thank heavens above, he thought piously and sincerely, this is to be an easy day once all the breakfasts are over. And perhaps the breakfasts would be light ones, after all the feasting of the night before.

The kettle boiled, the tea was brewing, he could wait no longer. He knocked on Cook's door. No answer, only a strangled snort as she turned over. He pounded, and then shouted, "Up! Up! It's near dawn and there's plenty to do! The fair opens today!"

That, at last, got through to her. In a moment she staggered out, unbrushed, unwashed, with her wrapper clutched around her. He handed her her cup of strong tea and she gulped it gratefully as she sank into her chair.

"Glory to God," she muttered. "There was a drop too much taken last night. Me mouth tastes like the bottom of a birdcage."

After a while she asked, "Where in the divil are the girls?"

"Give them a few minutes more. They jigged a hundred miles down here last night, after all the serving was finished upstairs."

"Glory to God," she said again. "And wasn't Pat the one with his mouth organ goin'? Near blew his lungs out. Pour me anither cup, there's a dear boy," she begged Simpson. "I'll not make it on one cup this morning. What's the weather?"

"Terrible. Still raining. The master'll be in a temper about that."

"The master and a million or two others. I'm glad I'm smart enough to stay home today. Bad enough to be stampeded to death without bein' stuck with umbrellas. Call the girls. We'll have to face this day, and the sooner the better."

Simpson rang for the maids and for the nannies. Adelaide and Nathaniel would be up soon and screaming if they were not fed on time. And Titus would be into some trouble, probably something loud. It would be better for them all if the exhausted household was awakened gently, with the smells of bacon and toast and coffee, not wailing babies.

Clementine did not need Simpson's bell to waken her. It was the Day! The day they had all waited for! Somehow in the excitement of the party for the Emperor and Empress, the plans for attending the fair had been pushed aside. There had been no time to think. And now here it was. May tenth was here!

She ran to the window to check on the weather. It was even worse than she had feared. Evidently it had rained all night long. The gutters were running full, and all up and down Spruce Street as far as she could see, banners and bunting and streamers hung in limp wet loops.

Miss Lamb yawned as the bell tinkled softly. "Shut the window, Clementine; it'll rain in. And let's dress quickly. We can help with the nursery trays, at least."

Once awake, Miss Lamb moved like lightning. No one would guess that she had danced for hours last night, and had who knows how little sleep. She pulled on her drawers, her vest, her camisole, her petticoats, stockings, shoes, all modestly under her nightgown. In one swish she dropped her nightgown to the floor as she pulled her blue dress over her head. And there she was, dressed.

It took Clementine longer, but not much. Her old schoolroom dress and everyday pinafore were good enough for now, and her tangled curls got only a quick lick with her hairbrush.

"Let Edwin sleep. It'll keep him out of trouble," ordered Miss Lamb. Clementine wanted Edwin up and thinking hard about how they could escape from the rest of the Tiptons and go off to the fair alone. Why had she let all these plans go until the last moment?

Suddenly there was the distant ringing of a single bell. That would be Independence Hall announcing sunrise. Sunrise, ha! And then, sun or no sun, every church bell and school bell and factory whistle in Philadelphia joined in a happy bedlam that made sleep impossible for anyone in town.

The weather would not stop the official opening of the fair, but thousands scanned the skies hopefully. The opening would certainly be more festive if the sun did break through.

And then about seven o'clock the wind shifted. A stiff breeze began to blow, the heavy gray overcast sky lightened, and the clouds began to tear apart and blow away.

"There's a patch of blue," screamed Clementine.

"Hush, child," said Miss Lamb, automatically, but

there was no real need for quiet. The bells and whistles had awakened everyone, and the whole house was beginning to bustle.

Breakfast in the day nursery was a confused affair. Clementine declared she was too excited to eat much, but really she was too nervous. The moment she was dreading finally came.

"Well," said Grandpa, "I won't have a special seat saved for me, but I trust I can accompany Miss Lamb and you two young devils as far as the fair grounds."

Luckily Miss Lamb missed this, for Titus set up a yell for more muffins. Edwin looked stricken, but kept right on eating.

"Grandpa," Clementine whispered. "Come out in the hall with me. There's something I've got to say." She looked so desperate that he followed her out of the nursery with his coffee cup still in his hand.

"If it's about how I made a fool of myself with the Emperor last night," he said, "I'll tell you right now I'm ashamed of myself."

"No, no! It's something — it's really serious — it's awful!" She blurted out the whole story of how she and Edwin had planned to go to the fair all by themselves.

"Don't you see? Mama and Papa think that Miss Lamb is taking us, and she thinks that they are, and now we can go with you, and that's next best to doing it all on our own, but if she finds out, she'll know we planned to go alone because we didn't know you were coming. She'll say she has to go with us, and she's been invited to sit in the press section with Mr. Hawkins and you can see for yourself how happy she is — and if anybody finds out, things'll be spoiled for everybody."

It was a confused story, but Grandpa Tipton seemed to get the drift. "Hmm," he said. "I can see we've quite a dilemma here. Let me think about it. And don't worry. Between us we can come up with something. Sshhh!"

Miss Lamb hurried out into the hall. "I'll help you dress, Clementine, and fix your hair, and then you are to sit absolutely still until your parents are ready to leave. Not a wrinkle, mind you. I am going to leave early. Mr. Hawkins is calling for me." She blushed self-consciously.

"Tell you what, Lambie-O," offered Grandpa. "Get the main trappings on her, and then run along. You can leave the rest to me. I'll watch both of them like a hawk."

Edwin and Clementine had never been dressed so fast.

"You look wonderful," exclaimed Miss Lamb. "You both look good enough to eat. Clem, take your hairbrush to Nanny McGregor; she'll get your hair into shape and tie your hat on just right. And now goodby; I must rush. Have a beautiful, beautiful day!" She hugged them both and dashed down the backstairs.

Mama and Papa and the house guests were still dawdling over breakfast, reliving the high points of the night before. It had been a smashing success, there was no doubt about it. Everyone remarked how charming and unassuming their royal highnesses had been.

"His Majesty did say one odd thing, though," Papa was saying. "As he left, he asked me to present his respects to my father, whose company he so enjoyed. Now whom do you suppose he mistook for my father?"

Clementine had come in quietly to check the sausage platter. Now that Grandpa had taken over the worry department she felt hungry again. She choked down a giggle and a piece of sausage and Mama looked around. "You look very sweet, dear; all but that dreadful hair! Do ask Miss Lamb to do something about it. The damp weather has made it wild as a bush."

Clementine made a hurried exit. What if Mama discovered that Miss Lamb had already left? She'd do her hair herself and then sit in the schoolroom until Papa and Mama were safely out of the way. It had been a mistake to call any attention to herself.

She brushed and brushed, this way and that, but no matter how she tried, her unruly curls would not settle down. And her beautiful new navy skimmer looked silly sitting high on a mess of ginger kinks. She was getting crosser by the minute. She wished she had short hair, like Edwin's — and without a second thought she reached for Miss Lamb's scissors. Slash! Slash! She whacked off the curls — and then stared in the mirror in a state of shock. There was a pile of red-

dish brown curls on the floor around her, and on her head — a rough, shaggy, uneven boy's cut!

The horror of what she had done so impulsively made her weak and lightheaded. Lightheaded? Yes, her head felt light and cool and free and — wonderful! She felt wonderful! She grabbed her new hat, slammed it on her head and tied it firmly under her chin. No one would notice, or if they did they'd think the curls were tucked up on top of her head.

The time of reckoning would come later, but for now she felt wild and free and happy! She tied the ribbons just in time, for Edwin poked his head in the door to say, "Hurry, the carriages are leaving, and then we can go! It looks as if all Philadelphia's already on the way. Come on, Grandpa Tipton's waiting."

There was going to be a mob, that was certain. Even on quiet Spruce Street there was a constant rattle and clatter of carriage and wagon wheels, and the sidewalks were full of people hurrying along toward Market Street where the horse-drawn streetcars and hacks were making their regular runs.

When they reached Market Street they knew a streetcar was out of the question. The cars were full, with passengers clinging precariously to the back platforms. Grandpa tried to hail a hansom cab and the drivers just laughed. Every one was already taken. Huge delivery wagons and smaller wagonettes were loaded. Dray horses strained under the load of the crowds they were carrying.

191

Every conveyance that had wheels, two or four, was on its way to the exposition. Owners of furniture wagons, vegetable carts, baggage vans and even hearses had been quick to fit their vehicles with rough seats and were prepared to make a profit.

Already streams of pedestrians, unable to find a ride, were hurrying across the bridges over the Schuylkill River, determined to get to the Centennial Exposition if they had to walk all the way.

Grandpa finally found one place in a butcher's cart, and squeezed the three of them in, much to the distress of the other passengers.

"We can't breathe already," screamed one excited old lady. "Driver, put these people off!" The driver was charging an outrageous fare of one dollar for the nine-cent run, and he just grinned and snapped his whip.

At the Girard Street bridge, pedestrians found they were making better time than the riders, for traffic had snarled so badly the vehicles were barely moving. Ahead were the towers of the Main Building, and ahead was a jostling, struggling crowd of thousands, pressed outside the fence, waiting for the gates to open.

Just outside the exposition grounds, along Belmont Avenue, were row upon row of flag-hung buildings — restaurants, hotels, saloons, beer gardens, coffee houses, a concert hall. And there was the Hall of Marvels, with pictures of the two-headed calf. The sidewalks were lined with stalls and the vendors added to the noise their shouts of "Peanuts! Get your Peanuts! Lemonade, fresh and cool! Have a roast potato while you wait! Get 'em hot, hot!" People were eating, for many had left their homes before dawn to be among the first through the turnstiles.

The new depot with its modern turnaround was thronged with visitors who arrived on the excursion trains from Baltimore and New York. Every thirty seconds a new train pulled in and added its passengers to the thousands of visitors already there.

Human beings were packed in like sardines in a tin, and though policemen were trying to keep order and were urging people to move along, there was no place for them to move. The din was unbelievable. The shouts of the frantic policemen, of the vendors, the blare of a calliope, the train whistles, the fearful oaths of the streetcar and carriage drivers trapped in the jam — the noise was overwhelming.

Grandpa cringed at the curses the drivers were hurling at one another, then shrugged and shouted in Clementine's ear, "You've probably heard worse in Culligan's kitchen!"

Clementine loved it all, the noise, the smells, the flags — not only the Stars and Stripes but the flag of each country represented in the exposition. From every post and pole, streamers blew in the breeze of the bright May morning. She leaned out of the wagon, not to miss a thing, and Grandpa kept a firm grip around her waist for fear she would topple out altogether.

Her hat was first pushed askew, then crushed, and finally fell back on her shoulders, secured only by the tight knot she had tied in the strings that morning.

"Let's get out!" shouted Grandpa. "We'll have better luck on foot." They could not hear what he said, but understood his motions and let go their grips on the rickety wooden plank seat. Other riders had the same idea, for the snarl of vehicles was getting worse, not better. A horse reared and an ice wagon rammed into them, interlocking the wheels, and as they stalled completely the ice wagon patrons began to jump out too.

All of a sudden there was a piercing scream, and even in the overwhelming din, Clementine knew the voice. There, face to face, as they jumped from their respective wagons, was Miss Lamb.

"Your hair!" she gasped. "Clementine, your hair!"

Clementine's fair-going dress was already mussed and stained, for the butcher wagon was none too clean, her new hat was smashed beyond repair, and her hair —

There was no time for explanations. The crowd gathered them up and swept them along. Clementine was too excited to be repentant. That would have to wait until later, along with the punishment she was sure to receive. She didn't care.

"Pooh to proper!" she shouted. "I'm liberated! I've got my women's rights!"

Chapter Seventeen

hey were jostled and shoved along Belmont Avenue. Between shoves Miss Lamb tried to ask, "What are you doing here? Where are your parents?"

"We're going to sit in the special guest seats with Grandpa," explained Clementine innocently. "See, he has the passes."

A bell rang, the signal for the turnstiles to open, and the horde of people stopped milling and jostling and poured along in one direction. Most had their fifty-cent pieces ready for admission, others waved guest tickets or press passes. Hundreds and hundreds of people surged through the gates and headed for the open space between Memorial Hall and the Main Building where the opening ceremonies were to take place.

Long before any of their little group could get there, others ahead of them had quickly taken places in the special seats and at the press tables, whether they belonged there or not. Mr. John Wanamaker, who was in charge of opening day arrangements, was vigorously weeding out the intruders and trying to seat those with legitimate passes. He had the help of his committee of volunteers, but even when they had routed the imposters, they discovered that far too many passes had been issued for the number of seats.

The reporters were thrashing angrily about, threatening to write accounts of the indignities they were suffering, but it did no good. Those who had secured seats at press tables were not about to give them up to rival newsmen. And the visitors who managed to reach a seat in the special section sat tight.

A man from the *Ledger* ran by, shouting, "Hawkins! Come on, follow me! There's room on the roof, and a grand view! This way! Come on!"

Mr. Hawkins tugged at Miss Lamb's arm.

"I can't," she said, almost weeping. "I can't leave these children. They're my responsibility."

"But I'm here," protested Grandpa. "We'll find a seat somewhere. I'll take care of them."

"You! You need taking care of yourself! Where were you when Clementine cut off her hair?"

"Miss Margaret," pleaded Mr. Hawkins, "if we don't hurry there won't be a place even on the roof."

"Move along, keep moving," said a policeman. "Stands are full, no more places, move along, move along!"

They were jammed against the base of one of the huge flying-horse statues. The streams of pushing,

196

shoving, joggling fair-goers held them pressed there, backs to the bronze base.

"You!" said Grandpa back to Miss Lamb. "You get along with your young man; you're interfering with his work! And as for these two — " he boosted Edwin and Clementine up onto the statue's base and jumped up to join them, right by Pegasus's rearing front hoof — "we'll stay right here out of harm's way, and I'll not let either of them out of my sight."

Miss Lamb still hesitated. A policeman, struggling through the mob, said, "Off the statuary! Be off with you. No one's to stand on the statuary, mister. Get down."

Grandpa Tipton roared fiercely, "Lay a hand on me and I'll have you arrested!"

The startled officer was shoved along, and Miss Lamb decided that Grandpa was serious. She took Mr. Hawkins's hand and ran, saying as she went, "You promised! Don't forget!"

The bases of the twin statues were soon crowded with people who were trying to get out of the press of the crowd, and before long the younger ones, the boys, anyway, began to venture higher. With absolute disregard for the dignity of the bronze muses of art and music and literature and the dance who were leading the winged horses, the boys used the goddesses as steppingstones and dug their toes into the folds of the flowing draperies to climb higher.

Clementine pushed her way among the climbers.

She had no mercy for anyone who was in her way, nor did any of the boys make way for her. It was each one for himself. Her fingers were stepped on more than once, but she persevered. The sculpture was an elaborate one, and the indentations in the long flowing mane of the horse, seemingly tossed by the wind, and in the deeply carved feathered wings provided footholds to make the climb possible.

Somewhere along the way Clementine had torn the ribbon from her smashed hat and had thrown it away. When she reached the top, bruised, breathless, perched right between Pegasus's ears where she could see everything, the boy who had pushed her most suddenly said, "Crimey! You're a girl!"

"Sure'n I am," she said, sounding like Sheila. "And would you like to make something of it?"

"Naw," he answered. "I'm not lookin' for a fight. I want to see the fair."

Edwin had taken another route up the side of the horse, a route that turned out to take longer. But eventually he made it, too, and Clementine moved over so that the two of them could fit snugly on Pegasus's head, with an ear for each one to hold onto.

Grandpa shouted up from below, "Hang on, you two idiots!" but he didn't sound worried. He could see that they were comfortably wedged in place. The muse of the dance was posed artistically with her knee bent, and it made a perfect little seat for him. He could keep an eye on the children just as he had prom-

ised. He was up out of the pushing of the crowd, and he could see most of what was going on.

From the top of the horse, Clementine and Edwin could see everything, up and down and everywhere. The fair grounds were not new to them, of course, for they had made the tour of inspection with Mr. Tipton on many a Sunday. But seeing huge empty buildings, only partly completed, was one thing, and seeing them finished, flag-bedecked and jammed with humanity was quite another. It was breathtaking. Directly ahead was the Main Building, with the platform built to hold the orchestra and the chorus of one thousand singers. From way up on the roof of this building someone waved in their direction. It surely was Miss Lamb, and they waved back, but they couldn't be sure that she could really pick them out in the mob, although Mr. Hawkins had brought binoculars.

Then if they turned their heads in the other direction, there was Memorial Hall and the platform where all the dignitaries were assembling.

The state buildings, each one flying its own state flag, stretched out on a long curved street, Crescent Avenue. There were Massachusetts, Connecticut, Michigan, New Hampshire, and all the rest of the twenty-nine state buildings standing proudly along the tree-lined promenade.

Then there were the foreign buildings, each as exotic as its builders could make it, with gilded towers and minarets and arches. But the buildings, exciting as they were, were nothing. It was the people who were the real excitement. The foreign diplomats were arriving on the platform, wearing brilliant uniforms with magnificent decorations. Their ladies were dressed just as brilliantly. The place of each group of foreign representatives was marked by the country's flag. Then in the midst of all this color were the members of the women's committee, seven hundred and fifty of them, all wearing white with silver stars gleaming on their breasts.

Ambassadors and judges, generals and politicians of every variety were there. Everyone who was anyone wanted a place on the dignitaries' platform. The committee of directors all sat together with their wives. Clementine could pick out Mama's blue dress and white straw hat with the red and blue cockade. Papa was not so easy to see. All the directors looked rather alike in their solemn black tail coats and silk hats.

As the various new arrivals came on the stage the multitudes cheered. Only those in the very front row of the crowd could see whom they were cheering, but all were so imbued with the holiday spirit that they cheered and applauded regardless of who was passing through the Avenue of the Republic, which was the name of the space between the two buildings.

By ten o'clock the sky was clear and the sun was bright and warm. The ladies on the platform fanned, but the ladies in the crowd were pressed in together too tightly for even the small motion of fanning.

Those who had brought umbrellas in case of more rain were glad to use them as parasols against the sun.

At exactly ten o'clock, Maestro Thomas, the orchestra leader, raised his baton and the orchestra began to play. It played the national airs of every country represented at the fair. The music was pleasant but it went on and on and on, and after a while the crowd that had been so quiet began to be restless and noisy. At last Maestro Thomas signaled his musicians to begin the Brazilian national anthem.

Right on time, Dom Pedro appeared at the front of the platform with his wife. His full title was Emperor Dom Pedro of Brazil, Prince of the Houses of Bourbon, Braganza and Hapsburg, but he preferred to be known simply as Dom Pedro. He was dressed more plainly than any man on the platform, as plain as the common people who had come to cheer him. And cheer they did! Longer and louder than they had cheered for any American or other foreign notables that day.

The roar of approval went on and on. Dom Pedro presented the Empress Theresa who bowed and smiled modestly. The cheers broke out again. Then the royal couple were seated to the right of the chair reserved for the President of the United States.

The crowd had started to push and jostle, with those behind pushing hard against the lucky ones near the front. There was such a crush that some of the spectators fainted and had to be carried away by the police.

Still others pressed forward, so that the mounted soldiers who were escorting the President and Mrs. Grant had difficulty clearing a path. There was such noise and confusion that no one quite realized that the President had arrived until the orchestra began to play "Hail to the Chief." Then there was another long tribute of cheering and clapping, which slackened off as the President bowed, shook hands with Dom Pedro, and sat down.

Clementine and Edwin had a clear view of all this, much better than if they had been sitting in the distinguished visitors section. They had been studying their programs for days, and when the orchestra began to play again, they knew it was the "Centennial March," composed by Richard Wagner.

The music rose gloriously, sometimes crashing and pounding like waves on a rock, at other times melodic and sweet. It was so stirring that Clementine found her heart pounding in her throat.

"The women's committee thought of that and paid for it," Clementine said proudly, nudging Edwin violently. "I'm glad I'm a woman."

"You watch out," he muttered. "You poke me again like that and I'll push you off. You won't live to grow up to be a woman or anything."

"Shut up!" said another of the boys straddling the horse's mane. "Let's hear what the old geezer's going to say."

The old geezer was the bishop who began to pray

aloud as soon as the music stopped. He prayed and prayed, covering every possible topic. Hardly anyone could hear what he said, but it was all faithfully reported in the newspapers the next day.

Then there was more music. The choir began to sing. The rich sound of a thousand voices rolled out over the crowd. It was so beautiful it made cold chills run up Clementine's spine, and she clung tightly to her horse's ear with one grubby hand while she dabbed at her eyes with the other.

Then it was time to introduce the President formally. General Hawley turned to President Grant and said, "I present to your view the International Exhibition of 1876!" There was a great burst of applause, quickly stilled as the people waited to hear what their president would say. His speech was short, and he ended by saying, "I declare the International Exhibition open."

The largest American flag ever seen was raised slowly above the Main Building. Dozens of foreign banners were unfurled and snapped in the breeze. The orchestra and chorus joined in the "Hallelujah Chorus" and were almost drowned out by the cheers from the hundred thousand spectators. Cannons thundered, chimes pealed, church bells rang, and whistles everywhere made it clear that the One Hundredth Birthday Exhibition of 1876 was in full swing.

As the chorus sang, the President and the several hundred guests filed from the platform and across the

Avenue of the Republic to enter the Main Building. The procession passed between the two statues of Pegasus, protected against the exuberant crowd by a line of soldiers and policemen.

"Hurrah for President Grant! Hip, hip hurray for Dom Pedro! Huzzah for the Empress! Hurrah for General Hawley!" Everyone was shouting and the dignitaries bowed and smiled as their names were called.

Papa and Mama passed close behind their majesties, and all of a sudden, carried away by the excitement of it all, a thin old voice shouted,

"Three cheers for Horace Tipton!"

Papa looked startled, and at the same time Clementine shouted, "No, Grandpa!" Papa turned, and there, just a little above his head, was Grandpa Tipton, perched like a pigeon on the lap of the muse of dance. Mama had heard that other voice, and even in the crowd she recognized it. She looked upward, saw Edwin and a shock-haired boy silhouetted against the bright sky, saw who the shock-haired boy really was, and pitched over in a dead faint.

The Empress had her smelling salts out in a flash, an obliging soldier caught Mama before she fell to the ground, another rescued her beautiful hat, and in a second or two she was upright again.

The procession moved on. It had all happened so fast that hardly anyone had noticed.

Only Clementine and Edwin and Grandpa. They had noticed.

"Race you down, kid," said the boy just behind her to Clementine. She shook her head and he shrugged and started to clamber down. Soon the statue was bare of all except Grandpa and Clementine and Edwin. The crowd had melted away to see the exhibitions and visit the restaurants and refreshment stands.

Miss Lamb and Mr. Hawkins hurried up.

"The view was simply glorious up there — beyond description!" she exclaimed. "You should have been up there with us."

"We certainly should have," said Grandpa. "We should have been on a roof a hundred miles away."

Miss Lamb looked from one to the other of their gloomy faces.

"Mr. Horace Tipton saw you," she guessed.

"Mr. Horace Tipton and Mrs. Horace Tipton," said Grandpa. "And Mrs. H. Tipton took one look at Clementine and fainted dead away. There'll be hell to pay tonight."

Chapter Eighteen

There *was no use* arguing or explaining. Miss Lamb did not even protest his language. They all knew Grandpa was right.

"Well," said Miss Lamb sensibly, at last, after she had pulled herself together. "We'll just have to let tonight wait. For now, we're here, and we should see all we can and enjoy ourselves. Where shall we go first?"

"I suggest the Women's Pavilion," said Mr. Hawkins. "Southley is covering the Main Building and the starting of the Corliss engine, and Jones the various state buildings, and I'm supposed to do a nice piece on the ladies."

The crowds had thinned and spread out by the time they reached the Women's Pavilion. Empress Theresa had been there to cut the velvet ribbon and start the engine throbbing, much as the Emperor and President Grant had done in the Main Building with the giant Corliss engine. They saw Miss Emma Allison, the engineer, a pretty young woman dressed neat as a pin in a brown and white dress, not looking at all like anyone's idea of a greasy, hardworking engineer.

From time to time she oiled something here or there, or adjusted a valve or checked a gauge. The rest of the time she stood there in her spotless white gloves and explained to the public how the power generated by her engine ran the sewing machines and power looms and the printing press that was clanking out souvenir copies of the magazine, "The New Century for Women."

The exhibition was not all machinery, not by any means. There were fine murals and paintings and large and small sculptures and needlework and tapestry and carved woods, all done by women, and even some etchings made by Queen Victoria herself.

It was really amazing, to see all these things gathered together in one lovely building. Clementine was proud and so was Miss Lamb, and it was plain the gentlemen of the group were surprised and impressed.

Then Grandpa took them all to lunch at a modest restaurant where they felt sure they would not run into the Tiptons or their guests or fashionable friends. Clementine and Edwin would have been glad to have their lunch from the various stands — a hot potato here, a bag of peanuts there, and orange phosphate at the famous soda fountain. But Grandpa complained that his feet were tired, and he needed a good sit-down meal.

All this had taken time, and Miss Lamb said, as they finished their dessert and rested their tired feet, "Aren't you glad we live in Philadelphia and can come

often? Imagine if we came from far away and had to try to see all this immense fair in a day or two?"

"We can come back often — every day, maybe," said Edwin enthusiastically.

All of a sudden the bright shining afternoon grew less so.

"Maybe you can," Clementine said. "I'll bet I spend the rest of the summer in my room. Maybe Papa'll lock me up for life."

"And I may be on my way back to England by tomorrow," Miss Lamb added.

"Never!" said Grandpa and Mr. Hawkins together. "We'll think of something," said Grandpa.

"Then we'd better get home and start thinking — and bathing," she said with a glance at Clementine's grubby face and hands.

"And hair cutting. Can't we improve on that haircut somehow, Lambie?"

By the time Mama and Papa and their house guests arrived home, Grandpa and Miss Lamb, with the nannies helping, had made quite a few improvements. Edwin and Clementine were scrubbed until they shone, and dressed in clean outfits. All four grownups had set to work on Clementine's hair, and after brushing and trimming and washing it, Miss Lamb pronounced it much better. It had to be cut quite short to even out Clementine's impulsive hacking, and now it clung to her head in a cap of short curls that dipped down a little longer in the back. It was startling, and not in the fashion, but it suited her and was somehow becoming.

Then there was nothing more to do but sit and wait until the carriages, their own and the rented ones, rolled up to the door. Shortly after that, they knew, the summons to the library would come. Clementine knew she should be nervous, unhappy, and repentant, but no matter how hard she tried, she could not be. She couldn't forget the excitement of the ride in the butcher's wagon, and how free she felt perched high on the bronze horse, and how lovely the music sounded. Best of all, how elegantly light and breezy her head felt. No hair ribbons, no tight clasps to keep her unruly curls in place, no snarls, no tangles — she loved it.

A sudden storm had blown up, and Clementine leaned out the schoolroom window to let the raindrops splash on her head. Miss Lamb nervously turned the pages of a book, Grandpa paced, Edwin spun the globe furiously on its stand.

At the back of the house and on the third floor they did not hear the carriages arrive or the bustle of guests. They were completely surprised when the schoolroom door was flung open. There stood Papa, and right behind him, Mama.

"What is the meaning of all this," roared Papa. And Mama was crying, "My baby, my precious, what were you doing up there, and your hair —"

And Papa, roaring even louder, "Why was the fam-

211

ily of Horace Tipton clinging to a stone statue —"

"Bronze," said Edwin, without thinking.

"And we weren't clinging; we were packed solid," said Clementine. Then she knew the interview had gotten off to a bad start.

Mama was dabbing at her eyes with her special exposition souvenir handkerchief and sobbing, "Up on a horse! With street urchins! And your hair, your beautiful, beautiful hair! Father Tipton! Miss Lamb! How could you?"

Miss Lamb and Grandpa Tipton started to speak together, trying to explain. All at once Clementine felt herself getting angry, angrier than she had been since the days of Mademoiselle. The hurts of many years seemed to boil up from someplace where she had put them away, as if she had packed her resentments tightly into a trunk and now the lid had burst open. Maybe the excitement of the day had helped free them, or her new pride in womankind. Something had released the catch. She did not know where her courage came from, but it was there.

"Stop it!" she stormed. "Stop it, all of you!"

They were all so surprised, they were silent. There was not a sound but the rain against the window and the slow ticking of the schoolroom clock.

"I'm sick of this," she yelled into the quiet. "Nobody ever called my hair beautiful until I cut it off. Nobody cared if it tangled and was miserable to comb and horrible to brush. It was always that 'ginger mop,

212

that kinky mess, that dreadful, dreadful hair, why couldn't you have inherited your mother's nice hair, too bad it's not like Adelaide's or Aunt Maude's' — or — or — even the trash man's! Anyone's but mine! Well, I'm tired of that, too. I'm plain and I'm homely and I don't look a bit like the beautiful Ashby sisters and I never will! I'm tired of hearing about the beautiful Ashby sisters! I'm me, can't you see? I'm a person, all by myself. I'm not just Mr. Horace Tipton's daughter. I'm me, Clementine Tipton. And I'm not just Olympia Tipton's daughter, either, to learn just enough to go out in society and behave nicely and no more than that. I've a brain, a good smart brain, and I'm going to fill it with all the things Miss Lamb can teach me, whether they're boys' studies or not. I'll grow up to be a woman, and I'll vote, too, just you wait, and I'll do all the exciting things women are going to do! And maybe you'll be proud of me and maybe you won't, but I will! I'll be me, and I'll be proud of it!"

It was quite a speech, considering that she hadn't planned to make a speech at all. Mama sat down suddenly in a chair. Papa's mouth hung open and he sort of rocked back on his heels. There was a long, long time when nobody said anything.

Clementine was crying, but it was an exhausted kind of crying, because she had put all her strength into her outburst, and now she was tired. She sobbed softly, and dried her tears on the hem of her dress as they fell.

Finally Grandpa said, "Not much any of us can add

to that, I'd say, except that things are going to be different around here. There it is, all laid right out for us to think about."

Papa said, and he seemed awed, "There are some things I must think about, it appears."

Mama said, "Baby, precious, I never realized, I didn't dream —"

Miss Lamb said softly, "I have a suspicion that when President Grant opened the fair today, much more than the United States came of age. I think we also witnessed the liberation of Clementine Tipton."

"No more tears now," said Grandpa. "She'll have her ups and her downs, but she'll make it. She's got good stuff in her, our Clementine, good stuff!" And then he added sensibly, "How about something to eat? We've all put in a long, busy day, and I'm starved. Has old Culligan any tasty royal leftovers for us, do you suppose? She'd better, or she'll hear about it from me."